WITCHING MOON

A Wild Hunt Novel, Book 12

YASMINE GALENORN

D1519546

A Nightqueen Enterprises LLC Publication

Published by Yasmine Galenorn

PO Box 2037, Kirkland WA 98083-2037

WITCHING MOON

A Wild Hunt Novel

Copyright © 2020 by Yasmine Galenorn

First Electronic Printing: 2020 Nightqueen Enterprises LLC

First Print Edition: 2020 Nightqueen Enterprises

Cover Art & Design: Ravven

Art Copyright: Yasmine Galenorn

Editor: Elizabeth Flynn

A Nightqueen Enterprises LLC Publication

Published in the United States of America

ACKNOWLEDGMENTS

Welcome back into the world of the Wild Hunt. We're at book twelve, and into the second story arc. The future is looming dark as Typhon rises and his emissaries begin to emerge. I love the world of the Wild Hunt, and am so grateful you do too. It's become a living, breathing entity in my thoughts and imagination.

Thanks to my usual crew: Samwise, my husband; Andria and Jennifer—without their help, I'd be swamped. To the women who have helped me find my way in indie, you're all great, and thank you to every one. To my wonderful cover artist, Ravven, for the beautiful work she's done.

Also, my love to my furbles, who keep me happy. My most reverent devotion to Mielikki, Tapio, Ukko, Rauni, and Brighid, my spiritual guardians and guides. My love and reverence to Herne, and Cernunnos, and to the Fae, who still rule the wild places of this world. And a nod to the Wild Hunt, which runs deep in my magick, as well as in my fiction.

You can find me through my website at Galenorn.com and be sure to sign up for my newsletter to keep updated on all my latest releases! If you liked this book, I'd be grateful if you'd leave a review—it helps more than you can think.

June 2020

Brightest Blessings,

~The Painted Panther~

~Yasmine Galenorn~

WELCOME TO WITCHING MOON

When you dance with Death, you have to be willing to roll the bones...

Still shaken from her run-in with the serial killer, Raven turns to a new and unlikely friend. But the Ante-Fae Trinity has dark secrets in his background, and he threatens to destabilize Raven and Kipa's relationship. When Trinity introduces Raven to a secret garden, it quickly becomes the place of nightmares. Will Raven's recklessness endanger her friends as well as herself? Or will the Wolf Lord and Raven's dearest friends not only put the nightmare to rest, but also drag Raven back from the edge of the chasm?

Reading Order for the Wild Hunt Series:

CHAPTER ONE

Even though it was a few minutes past nine, the sun was just beginning to dip below the horizon. Dusk was spreading out over the city as the echo of birdsong played through the trees, jumping from swaying bough to swaying bough. The firs and cedars were thick in the cemetery, along with a massive yew tree, its multitude of trunks weaving together to form a thick foundation rising out of the ground. The spirit in the yew tree was ponderous and ancient, watching over not only the cemetery but the entire area. Its energy leached into many a house and hearth for miles around.

I stood near a mausoleum, staring at the spirit who was hovering in front of me. She had been dead for so very long, but now she had woken up from her slumber and was staring down at me, pissed out of her mind. I took a deep breath and stepped back.

"Go back to sleep, old mother. Return to your grave, Lenora Maureen."

My voice rang clear and sure, as I forced as much

energy into the command as I could. I had the power to drive her back to the Phantom Kingdom. She couldn't move on, not until she let go of her anger and accepted her death, but I should be able to break her hold on the material world and send her packing.

However, Lenora didn't *want* to go. Instead of obeying me, she reared up, her misty form taking on substance. *Crap.* That's the last thing I needed. Ghosts who could take on corporeal form were the hardest to deal with.

"*Old mother*, back into your bed to slumber! Return to your grave." I intensified my focus and as I did so, the opening in the fabric of the Veil became visible. I could see the rip that led to the Phantom Kingdom as clearly as I could see the mausoleum.

The Phantom Kingdom was the world in which all realms intersected, and it stood outside of time and space. There, spirits who hadn't yet gone on to their rest or a new life wandered, looking for rips in the Veil so they could return to the world to which they were still so attached. The Phantom Kingdom also led to the Dreamtime, the spirit world, the astral realm, and other etheric altaverses. It was the universal realm that acted as a gateway to all other worlds, both physical and energetic.

I focused on the opening, softening my gaze. The rip didn't look like a natural portal, but rather like it had been *torn* open. Over the past few months, more and more tears like this had occurred, and they were directly related to Typhon's waking. He had not yet come into the physical realm, but he was awake and hiding out someplace in the Phantom Kingdom. As he spun out his plans, more breaches in the Veil were occurring. This was the fifth time I'd been called out by Herne and the Wild Hunt to drive angry ghosts back to the grave.

Feeling both irritated and exhausted, I resorted to one of the oldest tricks in the book. It was an old remedy, but effective. I opened my traveling bag o' magic and sorted through it until I found what I was looking for. *Goofer dust.* A variant of the usual hoodoo blends, I had mixed it with the specific intent to drive ghosts back through the Veil. First, I had blended a mixture of graveyard dirt, ground black pepper, silver filings, asafetida, and powdered raven's bones. Then I added clippings from my mother's hair—which she had willingly given to me—and charmed the whole mixture in Circle, invoking Arawn's energy into the cauldron.

Hand on my hip, I stared up at Lenora. She was rapidly taking form and it occurred to me that I'd better work fast, because by the look on her face, she was getting ready to dive-bomb me.

Frowning, I edged back a step as I tried to twist the lid off the jar of goofer dust. Apparently, that's all the impetus Lenora needed. I went flying through the air and landed on my butt at the base of a fern. The goofer dust went rolling to the side as I landed on a sharp rock jutting out of the ground.

"Motherfucking..." I groaned as I eased my tailbone off the rock, but froze as the spirit came barreling toward me again, this time in the shape of a misty ramrod.

"Oh no you *don't!*" I rolled to the side, grabbing up the jar of goofer dust. I came to a squatting position, keeping my eye on Lenora. The attack had disrupted her form, and she was now a scattered mist, but she was trying to gather herself together again—the mist was beginning to coalesce again.

Panting, I wrenched the lid off the goofer dust and waited for her to attack me again.

"Come on, *bitch*! You want a taste of me? Come on, try it again, I dare you!" I usually had respect for the dead, but not when they were trying to kill me. And with her attack, Lenora had crossed the line into my *I don't give a fuck* category. I would do whatever needed to send her back to where she came from.

As the sun vanished below the horizon, Lenora took on an ethereal glow, shimmering in the twilight. She was eerily beautiful, like a memory caught in time, transparent and tragic. Her face was vaguely skeletal—she had lost the vestiges of the woman she had once been. Chances were, she hadn't chosen to wake up. Chances were good that the Father of Dragons had been responsible for her waking. But even though it wasn't her fault, she was here now, awake and angry, and I was her current target.

"Time to go back to the grave, Lenora."

As she began to take form again, the mist thickening, fear rose in my throat. *She's just a spirit*, I whispered to myself. *You've tackled far harder jobs than this before.*

But then, before Lenora could attack again, I caught a glimpse of my hands. I was wearing fingerless lace gloves, but they couldn't hide my memories. My nails were shiny and new, they had grown in quickly, but there were scars all over my fingertips. I stared at them, feeling dizzy, and then...

I WAS STARING up at Pandora, chained to a metal table in a cavern, and nobody knew where I was. The blonde who had been so friendly to me at Fire & Fang was now leaning over me, gently stroking my face. But there were stars in her eyes and she swayed as I watched, the look on her face terrifying and cruel.

"I'm afraid this is going to hurt you a lot more than it does me, darling," she said, her smile turning feral. She held up a wicked pair of pliers. "We'll start easy, how about that? Now, buck up. I know you can handle this, lovely one. You're one of the Ante-Fae. You can handle far more than you think you can. I promise you that."

I tried to speak, but my tongue felt like cotton. She had charmed me so I couldn't say a word. I could scream, but I couldn't form words.

I struggled to speak, but I could barely open my lips. Frustrated, I let out a faint noise, the sound ripping out from my throat.

"Oh, love, don't thank me." A sneer replaced the smile. "Trust me, by the time I'm done with you, you'll curse me, you'll hate me, you'll fear me, and with every scream and every tear you shed, I'll feast on your sorrow. You'll never, ever forget me. I'll live in your dreams and your nightmares." She raised the pliers and moved away from my face, turning her attention to my left hand.

I felt her take my fingers, but couldn't see what she was doing. She had me shackled to the table, and the iron cuffs chafed at my wrists. Thank the gods I was Ante-Fae and not Fae or my skin would be blistered and burned by now. As it was, the iron would take its toll but it would take longer to do so.

As she held my index finger, I stiffened, realizing what

she was going to do. I shifted, fighting against the restraints, but to no use. The cuffs were rock solid.

"Don't worry, this won't take any time at all," Pandora said.

I tensed as I felt cold metal touch the tip of my finger. And then, the next moment, she laughed as a blistering pain registered through my finger. Before I could scream, she moved onto the next finger and by the time the screams ripped out of my throat, she was on the third. My voice echoed against the ceiling, ricocheting off the walls.

Pandora laughed and moved up to gaze in my face. "Delicious. You're absolutely delicious." She licked her lips, looking lascivious and wanton. As the fire spread through my hand and into my body, she returned to my side and took hold of the fourth finger.

Once again, the flames roiled inside...

LENORA CACKLED as she body-slammed me to the ground and I shook out of my memories. I rolled up, crouching low as I finally yanked the cap off the goofer dust. As the ghost launched another attack, I poured a mound of the dust in my hand and tossed it at her.

The dust hit her square in her face and confusion spread over her face as she went reeling back through the rip in the Veil. I held my hand up to the rip, focusing on smoothing it shut, and the tear sealed back together.

Lenora was back where she belonged. At least, for now.

I sat down on the grass, staring at the graveyard around me. It was quiet now, and although I could see a few spirits wandering the grounds, none of them seemed out of place or intent on causing trouble. I leaned back, bringing my knees to my chest. I wrapped my arms around my knees as the sound of birdsong echoed around me. As dusk settled, I gazed up at the emerging stars and began to cry. Around me, the spirits passed by, giving me muted looks of sorrow from their shadowy realm.

"I'M HOME," I said, opening the door. I had texted ahead. Kipa was constantly nagging me to let him know where I was and that I was all right. While I understood why, the truth was—his constant need for reassurance was beginning to bother me.

Raj came lumbering up to rub against my legs. While I had always loved him, lately we had grown closer. He kept an eye on my moods and it was as though he could sense I was lost in my thoughts again, trapped in my memories.

"Raven looks sad," Raj said. He stared up at me, his eyes wide and welcoming. "Is Raven in the bad place again?"

That was Raj's way of asking if I had slipped into another flashback. Ever since Pandora had kidnapped me, I found myself slipping into fugues, reliving the things she had done to me. And if Ember and Trinity hadn't come to my rescue, I'd be dead by now. I was all too aware of that fact. I prided myself on my ability to take care of myself. We Ante-Fae were hard to kill, but when a goddess took it into her mind to turn sadist, there wasn't much that mortals could do to stop her. And I had been reminded all too violently of my mortality.

"Raven's all right, Raj. Raven's home now." I knelt down and wrapped my arms around his neck, kissing him on the head. "How's Raj doing?"

Ignoring my question, Raj said, "Kipa misses Raven. Raven spend time with Kipa?" He gave me those big brown puppy-dog eyes that only gargoyles, cats, and dogs could muster.

I bit my lip, feeling torn.

Kipa had been nothing but wonderful since I had come home from the Healing Center in Annwn. But as much as I appreciated Kipa's protection, I chafed against it. Part of me wanted to retreat inside his arms, to beg him to go with me every time I left the house, just in case that psycho bitch was still gunning for me. But another part of me wanted to fight back, to prove that she wasn't ruling my life now.

I pressed my lips together, stroking the leather hide of Raj's back. He looked so worried that I finally smiled and nodded. "Yes, Raven will spend time with Kipa. Raven loves Raj."

"Raj knows Raven loves him. Does Raven love Kipa?"

Kipa and I were still dancing around those words, though I had the feeling he really did love me. But neither one of us approached the thought easily, and neither one of us took the declaration lightly. So the words remained unspoken, and I figured that—if they came—they would come in their own time. However, when it came to Raj, there was a fine line between love and like. He looked so anxious that I just nodded.

"Yes, Raven loves Kipa." And it was true, if I let myself admit it.

Satisfied, Raj wandered back to the living room where

he fired up the television. The lively sounds of *Acrobert and the Alphas* blared out, breaking the silence. I leaned back against the door, took a deep breath to steady myself, and then plastered a smile on my face and headed toward the living room where Kipa was waiting with Raj. He glanced up, his eyes lighting up.

"I'm glad you're home. Did you scare away the ghost?"

"She's back in the Phantom Kingdom, but it wasn't easy." I shrugged off the light jacket I was wearing and hung it on the coatrack. "I swear, there has to be a better way to deal with the situation. The gods are no closer to having an answer than they were last month, and things are getting very real, very fast."

Kipa scooted over on the sofa and patted the cushion beside him. "The gods are doing everything they can, but as long as Typhon's hiding out in the Phantom Kingdom, there isn't much we can do. To be honest, none of us know how to drive him back into stasis. There's a lot of talk and bluster, but not much to act on. Did you have any trouble tonight?"

"No, it was all pretty standard." I didn't want to tell him about the flashback. I was tired of having flashbacks, and I felt like I should be over them by now. Also, if I told him, he'd start to panic and then he'd try to make things better and we'd only end up in an argument.

"Is there any spaghetti left? I'm still hungry." Instead of sitting beside him, I headed toward the kitchen. I saw his smile fall away before I left the room.

He followed me into the kitchen, leaning on the counter as I rummaged through the refrigerator and found the cold spaghetti, neatly packed away inside of a plastic tub. Kipa had certainly gotten better at cooking over the past month or so, and he had also taught himself how to clean up after I had laid into him about leaving a sink full of dishes for me to do. I knew he was trying, and I wished I didn't feel so prickly.

"You want me to heat that up?" He moved to get a plate, but I shook my head.

"I like cold spaghetti. I'll just eat out of the container." I grabbed a fork before he could get it for me, and skirted him as I headed toward the table. He caught me around the waist though, pulling me in for a kiss. I stiffened, but let him kiss me on the cheek, then quickly disentangled myself and headed for the dining room.

"Do you want me to stay over tonight?" He followed me, but didn't sit down. Instead, he stood behind one of the chairs, leaning on the back of it. He was gorgeous, and he cared, and I hated that I really didn't want to be around him right now. I felt horrible because he was so good-hearted, but that was also why I didn't want him around right now. I was snapping at anybody over every little thing, and I didn't want to make him a target.

"No. Go ahead, I'm sure you must have things to do. It's so late that I think I'm just going to eat dinner and crash for the night." We had only had sex two or three times since I had escaped Pandora's lair. When anybody held me too tightly, even for a hug, I began to panic.

His shoulders slumping, Kipa let out an exhausted sigh. "Fine. I do have some errands to run." He paused, glancing at me.

I could feel the hesitation there and finally set down my fork. "I know you want to say something. I can tell. Please, just be honest."

"Do you even *want* me around? I've tried to give you

space, I've tried to help. I don't know what to do anymore. I don't know if you want me here, or if you just want me to leave. I'm never certain that you mean what you say nowadays. I don't know if you even still like me." The broken notes in his voice almost broke my heart.

Tears flecking my eyelashes, I turned to him. "I don't know what to say. I do care about you, more than you can possibly imagine. But I'm not coping very well with the aftermath of all this. I don't like being touched. Every time somebody hugs me, I feel like I'm trapped. I wake up in a panic if the blankets are too tight. I've…" I paused. I hadn't told him about the flashbacks yet.

"What? You're not telling me something."

"Kipa, I've been having flashbacks—I had one tonight while I was fighting that ghost and it gave her the chance to knock me over. I'm afraid every time I go out. I *know* I should be stronger than this. Hell, what she did to me *hurt*, but it wasn't as bad as what she did to the others. And I survived. I'm one of the Ante-Fae. I'm supposed to be *strong*. I'm supposed to be able to cope with things like this." I stared down at my spaghetti, not wanting to see the look of disappointment on his face.

Kipa pulled the chair out and slid into the seat. He didn't reach for my hand, but his voice was soft. "Raven, you may be one of the Ante-Fae, but you're still *young*. And you've never had to face anything like that before. Pandora didn't get as far with you as she did her other victims, but she was headed there. You have a right to be terrified. Neither I—nor anybody else—expects you to come through this without help. If you think that I expect you to just pretend it didn't happen, or be some strong silent heroine, you're totally wrong. I *do* want to be here for you. And I'm okay with not having sex right now. I'm okay with you not feeling capable of cuddling or hugging right now. What I'm *not* okay with is you keeping all of these emotions bottled up."

I hung my head. "Great. I feel guiltier than ever. No, really, you are being so good about this, and I feel like I've just turned into a total bitch."

"I wish you would talk to someone. I wish you would talk to Ferosyn. You have PTSD, and don't you even try to deny it. He could help."

It felt like I could barely breathe. I wanted to say yes. I wanted to ask for help. The trouble was, I wasn't quite ready. I felt like I was trapped in some horrible dream and every time I turned, there was something to remind me of that night. Whether it was the new teeth growing in my jaw where she had ripped out all my molars, or whether it was looking at the shiny new nails on my nail beds, or whether it was catching a glimpse of the scars on my body when I looked at myself naked in the mirror, Pandora was everywhere in my reality. Her reminders were every-where on my body. It didn't help that she was still alive, either. The gods were immortal, and I felt like I'd never be free of wondering if she was still out there somewhere, waiting to come after me again.

"I wish I could, too. I wish it was simply a matter of me saying yes, I want help. I just don't think I can talk about it yet, to anybody. Any therapist is going to want me to relive it, and I don't think I'm ready to go through it again."

"Raven, you're facing it every day," Kipa said. "You're coping with this alone, locked in your heart. Nobody can handle memories like yours without a little help." He paused, then let out another sigh and stood. "I'm here when you need me. I'll spend the night at my place, but if you call, I'll come running. You don't have to say anything, you don't have to do anything except just say the word—*just one word*—and I'll be here. Meanwhile, I'll give you some space."

"I'm sorry," I said, tearing up. "I'm so sorry."

"You have nothing to be sorry for." Kipa slipped on his leather jacket, and headed for the door. Pausing, he looked back over his shoulder. "I'm not letting you push me away. I know that's not what you want, and I know you're trying to protect me from your moods. Trust me, I can handle far more than you think, and I've seen far worse. I'm here when you need me." And with that, he patted Raj on the head and took off out the door.

I pushed back the container of spaghetti, trying to steady my breath. I wanted to cry. I wanted to scream. I wanted to break things and throw things. It was like I had an inner spring that was coiled so tightly that it was ready to break. Finally, I managed to calm down. I stared at the table until I could breathe again, then began eating again.

CHAPTER TWO

My phone rang. At first I thought it was the alarm, trying to jog me out of sleep, but then I noticed the ring tone was different. It wasn't my usual Marilyn Manson wakeup call. I forced my eyes open and rolled over in the bed, grabbing my phone up from where it was on the opposite pillow. It was probably Kipa, checking in on me. But when I glanced at the number I realized that it was Llew, one of my best friends. Groggily, I answered as I propped myself up on a pillow, leaning over it as I attempted to pry the gunk at the corners of my eyes.

"Hey, Raven, I'm glad I got hold of you." Llew sounded somewhat strained, and I knew it was because I hadn't been down to the shop since I had gotten home from Mount Bracken. I had tried a few times, but I just couldn't bring myself to go. Llew had been playing phone tag with me for several days now, and I finally decided that I had to answer him.

"Hi, Llew, sorry I haven't been around much lately. I've been…" How should I say it? I've been freaking out inside? I've been having flashbacks? I've been hiding out away from anybody and everybody?"

"Busy, right. That's what Kipa said the last three times I called your house phone."

That reminded me that I had planned to have the land-line removed. I jotted a note to myself on the pad of paper on my nightstand, then decided honesty was best.

"I just haven't felt up to coming in. I'm sorry that I haven't phoned to talk to you about it." I paused, realizing that there was nothing more to say.

"That doesn't surprise me. What *does* surprise me is that you couldn't talk to me about it. We've been friends for years, Raven. A lot of people rely on you for consulta-tions. If I can just give them a timeframe, everything will be all right. But I've had to tell them time and again that I don't know when you're coming back."

I frowned, feeling slightly attacked. "Llew, you *do* know everything that happened to me up on that moun-tain, don't you?"

"Of course I do. Unless you held something back. And it's fine that you're not coming in right now. Just talk to me and give me some sort of timeframe."

I frowned. "Why can't you just tell them I'll be there later? That I'm on vacation or something?"

"Because even if you were on vacation you would have a return date. Humans aren't like you or me. They need a frame of reference." He waited for a moment and when I didn't answer, he asked, "You *are* coming back to the shop, aren't you?"

I stared at the wrinkles in the sheets, trying to decide whether I wanted to bother ironing them. I decided that it wasn't worth it, given I'd just mess up the bed again.

"Raven, are you there?"

I shrugged, nodding. Then, realizing he couldn't see me, I said, "Yes, I'm here. I'm nodding. But Llew, I don't know when I can come back."

There was silence on the other end of the line for a moment, then Llew said, "Raven, we've known each other for quite a while, haven't we?"

I nodded, saying, "Yeah, we have. You're one of my best friends."

"And being one of your best friends, I like to feel that I can say just about anything to you, can't I?"

I stiffened, then whispered, "Of course you can."

"All right. I'm saying this with love. Get your damned ass down here and get back to work. The last thing you need right now is to sit at home, dwelling on what happened. I think you should go to therapy. Kipa thinks you should go to therapy. Even *Ember* thinks you should go to therapy. But you won't. Fine. You don't want to. But for the sake of the gods, keep yourself busy. Don't give yourself time to think." His words were caring but stern. I could practically see his expression now. Llew and I had known each other for many years, and he truly was one of my best friends.

Part of me wanted to snap back at him, but I knew he was right. I didn't want to go in—I didn't really want to do anything. But I couldn't just sit here forever.

"All right. I'll come down tomorrow."

"No, you'll come down *today*. I know that you don't have any plans. I know you. Normally you'd be booked to the brim with things to do, but ever since Pandora kidnapped you, you haven't done a damn thing that you haven't had to. I know that sounds harsh but it's true, isn't it?"

I glared at my phone for a moment, then said, "I'll be down in an hour or so." As I punched the end talk button, part of me was grateful that Llew felt he could talk to me that way. Because it meant he cared.

It was warm enough that I scrambled into a short black petticoat, then a purple sundress with a swirly skirt. I added a black patent leather belt, and platform Mary Janes. I never went out in public without my makeup so I managed to get eyeliner and some violet lipstick on, and I pulled my hair into a high ponytail. As I walked into the kitchen, Raj was sitting by his dish, looking woefully at the empty plate. He glanced up at me, his eyes lighting up.

"I'm late for breakfast, aren't I?" I asked, kneeling to pick up his plate. He followed me into the kitchen where I pulled out a clean dish and opened a large can of cat food into it. "How about a special treat today?"

"Raven feel better?" Raj asked.

"Yeah, I guess. Raven's going down to Llew's shop today to read the cards. Will Raj be okay here?" I had beefed up my wards, adding a magical security system as well as a physical one just in case Pandora took it into her head to pop into my house. One of my biggest fears was that she would show up and retaliate by hurting Raj.

"It's good for Raven to go to the shop. Raven's been alone too much lately." Raj leaned against me, then sniffed at the plate as I carried it to the dining room.

"Raven's okay, Raj. Don't worry about her, okay?" I

didn't like that he was so fixated on my moods. I didn't want him unhappy.

"Raj always worries about Raven, just like Raven worries about Raj. Raj loves Raven." He gave me a quick look before he turned his head back toward his plate.

I leaned down, giving the gargoyle a big hug around his neck and kissing him firmly on the forehead. "And Raven loves Raj. Always remember that, okay?"

"Okay," Raj said, falling to his breakfast.

I gathered my things and, for the first time in weeks, set the security alarms and headed toward the Sun & Moon Apothecary.

LLEW WAS WAITING for me when I entered the shop. He owned the Sun & Moon Apothecary in downtown Redmond, a shop primarily for witches, but in actuality, a large contingent of customers came through, everyone from human pagans to sorcerers to little old ladies who wanted me to read their cards. I had developed a strong clientele and while the money never hurt, I liked that I had also developed a friendship with some of them.

Maxine, one of my regulars, was waiting for me when I arrived. Seated at the table near the window, she was patiently riffling through a knitting magazine. I waved at her, then walked over to Llew.

"So, are you mad at me for talking to you the way I did?" He leaned across the counter to place a quick kiss on my cheek. Llew's husband owned the coffee shop next door, and both Jordan and Llew had become good friends over the years.

"Yes. But you're right. Things feel like they're falling apart right now. I feel adrift. One minute I'm lonely and wanting Kipa by my side, the next minute I'm angry and yelling at him. I don't want to be like this, Llew." I gave him a pleading look.

"We'll talk after you read for Maxine. She's been waiting for several weeks to have you read her cards. Go on now, and I'll get some coffee for you over at Jordan's. What do you want?"

I wasn't really that hungry, but coffee did sound good. "A triple-shot caramel latte, please. And if he has any caramel sticky buns, one of those."

"Sure thing." Llew grabbed a twenty out of the till and headed out. I wandered over to where Maxine was waiting.

"Hey." I sat down on the opposite side of the table and pulled out my cards. "It's been awhile."

As I set up my cards and crystal ball, Maxine watched me from over her magazine. She was in her seventies, human, and sharp as a tack. Sometimes it was hard for me to believe she was as old as she said she was. She didn't look seventy-five, and she seldom acted it. But there was a wise woman feel to her, and I wondered if she had ever practiced any sort of magic in her life. She had the feel of the crone, even though she didn't look old enough to be one.

"It's been awhile since you've been down here," she said and I could feel the question behind her words.

I merely nodded, then lit the candle sitting by the side of the table. It was a large pillar candle on a three-foot tall pedestal. The comforting scent of sage rose to waft around us, clearing the air.

"Shall we get started? What would you like to ask the cards today?"

Maxine set her knitting to the side and straightened in her chair. She rested her elbows on the table, leaning on them as she stared at me. "I'm facing a dilemma with my daughter."

I knew that Maxine had been married at one time, but I didn't realize she had children. "You have a daughter?"

She nodded. "I was married twice. Neither marriage lasted very long. My daughter is from my first husband. She's forty-six, and I'm worried about her. She recently quit her job, and she's blowing through her savings. I asked her if she was going to look for a new position but she said that she's tired of working and needs a break. Her job was never that stressful, though. I'm not sure what's going on, but I can't help but feel that she's making a mistake, if not more than one. I'm worried she's headed toward a bad end. Can you give me any insight into what I should do, if anything?"

I shuffled the cards, frowning. As I laid them out, several cards jumped out at me as though they were shining around the edges. The eight of chalices, the seven of chalices, the ten of wands, and the prince of athames.

"Is your daughter involved with a man who's an intellectual sort? He might be born under the sign of Gemini or Libra or Aquarius, although I tend to think either Gemini or Libra would be the most likely."

Maxine gave me a nod. "Darrell. He's a Gemini, and they been together for about four months now. Maybe five. I don't like him very much. The man has a nasty sense of humor. What he calls a joke, I call attacking others. He's been gaslighting my daughter, and I've tried to talk to her but she doesn't want to listen."

That told me a great deal. "Looking at the cards, I hate to say it but I think he has substance abuse issues. I also think he's an emotional vampire. He's draining her dry of energy, and she has started to feel unsettled and unsure of herself. Is he living off of her?"

Maxine slapped the table. "*I knew it.* She tried to tell me that she's not supporting him, but he's always over there eating her food, he stays at her place, and I know that she's buying too much booze lately. She's never been a drinker but all of a sudden she's buying wine by the case. And I thought…" She paused, then lowered her voice. "I thought I saw a bottle of pills on the table the other day, and there was no prescription label, and they sure didn't look like vitamins to me."

I bit my lip. I didn't like throwing people under the bus, but there was no doubt in my mind about this guy. "Darrell is leeching off of her in a number of ways. He's draining her self-esteem, and I think he's trying to cut off her connection to you. Emotional abusers do that. He also has a substance abuse problem. Probably alcohol, since you mentioned it. Do you know why she quit her job?"

Maxine shrugged. "I asked her, but she wouldn't answer. Or rather, she gave me a roundabout answer that she just 'needed some downtime,' that 'things at work were getting a little too stressful.' My daughter was up for a big promotion and she blew it. Six months ago, you couldn't pry her away from that job. I thought maybe someone at work might be sexually harassing her, or maybe they gave her too many things to handle. But now… I think it was Darrell who convinced her to quit."

I pulled another couple cards from the deck, but they indicated home life, and this time I got the king of athames. "Yeah, I think you're right. I think Darrell told her to quit her job. Men like this like to control every aspect of their partners' lives. I've seen it in straight relationships and I've seen it in gay relationships. I've seen it in marriages, affairs, and dating. When you visit them, or when they come visit you, does he seem uneasy, like he's trying to keep secrets?"

She nodded. "Actually, yes. My daughter used to come over at least twice a week. We had dinner together one night every week. But since Darrell came into the picture, we've only gotten together twice. Last time they were supposed to come over she called and made the excuse that she had a cold and wanted to stay home. I offered to come over and look after her, but she said Darrell would take care of her. I tried once more, but she blew me off again. Am I imagining things, or is he interfering in our relationship?"

I nodded, pulling yet another card. The Hermit came up. "He's trying to cut off her connections, and yes, that's very common in abusive relationships. She needs to get rid of him or he's going to drain her bank account and probably worse. She's already questioning her self-esteem and her place in this world. And if she's sick, chances are he's not taking care of her the way she needs to be."

Maxine hung her head, shaking it lightly. "All right, I believe everything you're saying. It fits the pattern. What can I do? How can I help my daughter escape from the situation?"

"Unfortunately, your daughter is an adult. She has to make her own decisions and this is one of those life journeys that will be a crossroads for her. If she doesn't get rid of him, her life's going to go downhill from here. But if you try to force him out, she'll resent you because he's already got her under some semblance of control." I paused, thinking over what advice I should give her. Then it occurred to me that we were in a magic shop, and surely Llew had something that might help the situation.

"As soon as Llew gets back from the coffee shop, I want you to tell him about the situation and ask him if there's anything he can recommend. Meanwhile, let me pull an advice card." I focused on the cards, tapping the back of the deck three times before cutting it in half. As I turned the top card over, the magician appeared.

I smiled. "Yes, that's the best thing you can do. The magician is not only communication and quick thought, but he represents the magical arts. Talk to Llew. I think he can help you better than I can."

"Oh, don't worry about helping. You already have. Now I know what I'm facing. And you can't fight an enemy that you don't understand."

That moment Llew entered the shop again, a tray of coffee cups in one hand and a bag of what I assumed were pastries in the other. He had bought a cup of coffee for Maxine as well, and she gratefully accepted it. I set my caramel latte to the side, then took the bag of pastries from him.

"Let me put these on a plate while you talk to Maxine. She needs magical advice." I carried the pastries back into the break room, where I found a tray and arranged them neatly. I had to admit, Llew had been correct. Coming down to the shop had made me feel better, and even though I hadn't been able to solve Maxine's problem, the fact that I had managed to make inroads on it sparked a feeling I hadn't felt in a while. I actually felt *useful*.

I carried the pastries out to the counter and set the tray next to the cash register. Llew was deep in conversation with Maxine, showing her several herbs and a couple of potions. I wandered back over to my table, carrying a maple bar with me, and sat down to eat. As I sipped my latte and watched the flurry of passersby outside the window, I realized that I was breathing easier. I had just finished my maple bar and was licking my fingers when Moira Ness entered the shop. She waved at me, looking lighter than she had in ages.

Moira had been coming to me for a long time, but it had only been recently that I had helped her sort out a trauma that she hadn't wanted to face. For a long time she had continually asked for information on her late sister's spirit, but I had a feeling that she'd been able to finally let it go by the look in her eyes.

I motioned to the chair and she sat down. "It's good to see you."

She smiled and glanced over at the pastries. "Are those free for the taking?"

"Of course. I don't know if Llew has made the coffee for the shop yet or not, though."

"I've already had three cups this morning, I'd better take it easy for now." Moira headed over to the pastry tray and selected one, setting it on a paper plate. She picked up a napkin and returned to my table. As she stared at her plate, I had the feeling she wanted to say something.

"Is everything all right? Is there something you need to tell me?"

"I don't want you to be mad, but I pestered Llew until

he told me why you've been out." She reached across the table and took my hands in hers. "My dear, I'm so sorry."

I knew she was just expressing sympathy, but I cringed and pulled my hands away. I didn't want to talk about Pandora. I didn't want to talk about what had happened to me. But at the hurt look on her face, I had to say something.

"I'm all right. Thank you for your concern. But truly, I'm okay. Now, what can the cards answer for you today?" I picked them up, forcing a smile to my face.

Moira stared at me for another moment, then relented, leaning back in her chair. "Why don't we go with something easy this time? I'm entering a flower arranging show and I joined a gardening club. Can you give me any idea of how that's going to go?"

And so I read the cards for her, and after she left three more people came in who had been waiting for me to return. By the end of the day I was exhausted, but for the first time in weeks I felt more like myself. Llew had been correct. I needed to get out of the house more. I sucked in a deep breath, then stood and began loading my back-pack. When I was ready to go, I texted Kipa and asked him to come over for the evening. Maybe, just maybe, I would be able to get my relationship back on track too.

CHAPTER THREE

WHEN I TEXTED KIPA, ASKING IF HE COULD COME OVER, HE texted me back saying that he would be held up until at least nine P.M. I told him I'd see him then, and headed back to my car. I had gotten rid of my Toyota Camry because every time I saw it, I couldn't get rid of the memory of Pandora flagging me down for help. For some reason, I had thought nothing of seeing her on the side of the road, and had slowed down on my way home from Ember's. She got in the car, saying very little. All the way to my house I had felt like something was wrong, but I couldn't seem to frame the question of why. And then, as we pulled into my driveway, everything had become a blur. I didn't remember anything else until I woke up in the cavern under Mount Bracken.

So I had traded in my Camry, which I had loved, for a Subaru. It wasn't exactly my style, but it was a sturdy car, with plenty of room for Raj in the back, and the best thing about it was that it didn't send me into a flashback when I saw it.

I arrived home, holding my breath until I made it into the foyer. Locking the door behind me, I was relieved to see the alarms were still functioning and hadn't been triggered. Raj was sitting on the sofa, watching TV, and he bounded over to greet me.

"Raven have a good day? Raj watch TV and eat cookies." He beamed at me.

Gargoyles were incredibly intelligent, but in a vastly different way than humans, and Raj's interactions with me often made me wonder if he had been stunted developmentally. Given that a demon had owned him from birth, there was a good chance that he had experimented on my poor Raj, but whether Raj was normal for a gargoyle or not didn't matter. I loved him because he was my buddy and friend. And I'd take care of him until the end.

I gave him a hug, kissing him on the forehead. "Raven had a good day. Raven enjoyed seeing Llew in the shop again. Did everything go okay here? Raj was all right today?"

Raj nodded, his head bouncing like a bobble-head toy. "Nobody came. The ferrets made a racket." He wandered back to the TV. Raj was a couch potato, and he loved TV with a passion. He'd watch anything and everything, just so long as it was happy and upbeat. I had recently found him watching *Musical Weddings*, a show where four couples spent twelve weeks in trial marriages with each other—much like musical chairs. Every two weeks they changed spouses. The cat fighting and jealousy were over the top, but Raj watched happily, hoping for a happy ending for everyone. I didn't bother telling him it was probably rigged. He enjoyed rooting for the couples he thought were the underdogs.

I wasn't particularly hungry, but I wandered into the kitchen anyway, finding a bag of chips that I had hidden behind some canned beets. Raj hated canned beets, and I knew he would never look there even if he managed to get the cupboards open. I poured the chips into a bowl and carried them into the living room to share with him.

Raj began to describe who the different couples were, along with a few odd comments that led me to wonder if he'd been watching *Runway Divas*, a virtual fashion show, lately.

"Piper's dress looks like she found it in a thrift store," he said offhandedly, doing his best imitation of RuPaul. "And *honey*, that ain't good."

I swiveled, staring at him. "Um...okay. What makes you say that?"

"Dennis said it, and Raj likes Dennis. Raj wants Dennis and Piper to get married." Then he shushed me, and went back to watching intently.

A chime sounded, announcing that someone was texting me. I glanced at my phone, wiping my hands on a paper towel to get the oil off of them. It was from Trinity.

HEY RAVEN, DO YOU WANT TO CATCH A DRINK AT THE BURLESQUE A GO-GO?

I glanced at the clock. It was barely six. Kipa wouldn't be over for three hours. I CAN MEET YOU FOR A COUPLE OF HOURS. SEE YOU THERE IN TWENTY MINUTES.

I stood, turning to Raj. "Raven has to go out for a couple hours. She'll be home by eight-thirty. Kipa is coming over later tonight to spend some time with Raven and Raj. Raj will be okay?" I handed him the bowl of potato chips.

He nodded, still staring at the TV. I touched up my makeup and made sure that my hair was brushed, then slung my purse over my shoulder. Placing my foot on a chair, I tested my dagger sheath that was firmly buckled around my thigh, sliding Venom back into it. Venom was my blade, and she had a poisonous bite. We worked well together, and I never went out without her now, although I caved when it came to the Sun & Moon Apothecary. Llew had specifically asked me not to wear weapons in the shop, and I respected him enough to abide by his ruling. When I got there, I took Venom off, stowing her in my purse, peace-bound. When I left, I made sure she was firmly against my thigh again.

I checked to be certain the wards were activated, and I also double-checked the magical security system. Then, waving to Raj, I locked the door behind me and headed to my car. The motion sensors flashed on the moment I set foot on the porch. It cast a bright light across the drive-way, and as I headed for my car, I saw Trefoil and Meadow sitting outside in their yard. I wandered across the street to say hello.

"Hey, what's hanging?" I had come to like them, and I actually felt more secure with their presence in the neighborhood. They belonged to the paramilitary branch of LOCK, the Library of Cryptic Knowledge. I had recently discovered that LOCK was secretly run by the Force Majeure, the most powerful magical organization in the world. That Trefoil and Meadow O'Ceallaigh were in the military branch gave me more of a feeling of security.

Meadow looked up, red hair sparkling under the

evening sunlight. She and Trefoil were brother and sister, members of the magic-born, and although I had never seen them in action, I knew just how powerful they could be.

Standing, Meadow stretched and yawned. "Hey, we're fine. How are you?" She frowned, and once again I felt like I was in the spotlight. I was beginning to hate the fact that so many people knew what had happened to me. It wasn't that I wanted to keep it a secret, it was just that everywhere I turned, somebody either wanted to help me or tiptoe around me.

"Fine. I went down to read at the shop today. I'm going to be gone for a couple hours right now, so if you're around, would you mind keeping an eye on the house? I have the wards set and I also have the security system set, but I'd still feel better if I knew someone was paying attention. I should be back around eight-thirty."

She nodded, her expression grave. "We'll be around. We decided we wanted to do some star watching tonight, so we should be out here all evening. Have fun and we'll see you in a while."

Trefoil waved at me as I murmured "Bye" and headed back to my car. As I drove out of the neighborhood, everything felt so normal, and yet so different. And I knew we wouldn't be back to normal for a long time, if ever.

THE BURLESQUE A GO-GO was jumping, and I waved at the bouncer as he motioned me through. I was a regular, friends with the owner, and everybody who frequented the nightclub knew me. As I entered the bar, the lights fell away and a dark ambience glittered over the room. The Vulture Sisters were up on stage dancing, a Gothic belly dance that made me think of birds of prey—which they actually were. They were Ante-Fae, like me, but they were much more predatory and they made no move to hide the fact.

I glanced around, looking for Vixen. Vixen was the owner of the club, and they were sitting over in a corner chair as usual with Apollo—their Golden Boy—by their side. Tonight, Vixen was wearing a top hat, a pair of leather pants, and a slinky shirt open to their waist. Gender-fluid in the truest sense of the word, Vixen shifted form each day, depending on what they felt like being.

I headed over to the table, motioning to the waitress as I did so. "A Blueberry Warble, please." The milkshake was fortified with blueberry liqueur, and it was the newest thing on the menu. It came quickly.

"Raven, my love. Sit down." Vixen pushed the chair out from the table with their foot. They never flirted with me unless they were in male form, which I found interesting.

"I can only stay for a couple of hours. Trinity's meeting me here."

A shadow passed across Vixen's face. "Are you still hanging out with the Keeper of the Keys? He's not healthy for you, Raven. While he may have saved your life, he's still a form of Mesmer, and you shouldn't trust him."

I let out a sigh. Lately, every time I got together with Vixen and Apollo, they tried to talk me out of hanging out with Trinity. They didn't like him, and Vixen only tolerated his presence in the bar because of me.

"I don't see what's wrong with him. And if you don't tell me, I'll never know what it is you have against him. Trinity's in a class on his own, I grant you that. But aren't we all? All of the Ante-Fae and the Exosan?"

The Exosan were members of the Ante-Fae who liked to interact with humans. I was one of them.

"It's not that I don't *like* him, but chaos follows him as sure as frost follows the autumn. And Trinity can't control his chaos. And sometimes I think he revels in the fact that it goes awry." Vixen narrowed their eyes, leaning forward. They lifted their drink and took a slow sip from it, then deliberately set it down and held out their hand to me. I placed my fingers in their palm and they wrapped my hand with their warm one. "You should talk to Herne about Trinity. I'm sure he'll have more information that he's willing to share, but let it be known that I go on record as saying I don't like that you hang out with him. I imagine that your lover isn't exactly thrilled with the idea either?"

While Vixen was polyamorous, they knew that I wasn't. And they knew Kipa well enough to know that he didn't like sharing his partners.

"I'll deal with it in my own way. We're fine. Kipa understands that I'm going through something that you can't possibly know anything about. I'm dealing with memories that—"

"Don't start with me, *girl*," Vixen said, lowering their voice. "You know very little about my history. Don't spout off at the mouth until you know more. I'll stop pressing you about Trinity, but don't say I didn't warn you."

I was about to answer back when I noticed the door open and Trinity entered the nightclub. I stood. "Since

Trinity's presence causes you so much concern, I'll talk to him at a different table. See you later, Vixen. You too, Apollo."

Apollo merely nodded, but Vixen shook their head, scowling.

As I headed across the dance floor, weaving through the throng of dancers and partiers, I couldn't help but wonder if Vixen was right. Was Trinity dangerous? Could I trust him? I still knew very little about him, even though he had saved my life and we'd started hanging out together more. But there was something about him—something unfettered and free that made me want to run by his side. I wasn't that attracted to him, not on a physical level, but his fearless attitude did appeal to me, and for now, it felt just what the doctor ordered.

TRINITY LEANED AGAINST THE BAR, waiting for me.

"Raven," he said, motioning to me, and I slid into his embrace, giving him a peck on the cheek before I sat on the bar stool next to him. We had only known each other for a short time, but it felt like forever. Trinity was carefree, and he wasn't attached to anyone, although he did seem to care for a number of people. Unfettered, Trinity came and went as he pleased.

"Hey Trin." I sighed, glancing back at Vixen and Apollo, who were both watching us. "They're not happy about you being here."

"Not my circus, not my monkeys. I pay my tab, and I don't cause any brawls. If Vixen doesn't like me, they can toss me out on my ass, but I'm not going willingly just to save them some trouble."

He arched one eyebrow and I grinned. The dark liner around his eyes was natural and gave him a roguish, Goth look, not quite the raccoon-mask look, but close. He had black hair that fell down his back in a braid, and he was wearing a pair of black leather pants and a black velvet jacket with ruffled sleeves and gold military buttons. Formfitting to the waist, the lower part of the coat flared out, and there were gold and blue stripes on the shoulders. Trinity was like a combination rock star–pirate in his style, flamboyant as hell but it came naturally to him, so it didn't seem affected.

I had been hesitant to ask, but finally I decided that I needed to know. I trusted Vixen and Apollo, and I couldn't figure out why they didn't like Trinity.

"I need to know why Vixen doesn't like you." Finishing my milkshake, I motioned to the bartender and ordered a glass of red wine.

"They have their reasons," Trinity said, his answer far from reassuring.

"Are you going to tell me those reasons?"

He shrugged. "I might. Why do you want to know?"

"Because Vixen and Apollo are my friends, and their opinions matter to me. If they don't like you, they've probably got some reason and I'd like to know why."

"Why didn't you ask them?"

"Because I want to hear your side of the story first. There are always two sides to a story. I like you, Trinity. And I owe you big. You helped Ember save my life."

"Not necessarily. When you think about it, Merlin saved all of us. I was just along for the ride. I'm glad you survived, though." He gazed at me, his eyes clear. That was one thing I could count on, Trinity almost always told the truth. He might be a master of persuasion, but he didn't lie to get what he wanted.

"Just tell me, all right?"

He played with his glass for a moment, then pushed it back toward the bartender. "Another, please." Looking at me again, he said, "Raven, I'll make you a bargain. I'll think about telling you why Vixen and Apollo don't like me, if you'll come exploring with me. I found something." He held up a keychain, dangling a copper key from the end. By my estimation, the keychain had more than one hundred keys on it. It rattled as he toyed with it. While I knew it had to be heavy as hell, he treated it as if it were light as a feather. That's one thing about the Ante-Fae, we were all fairly strong.

I caught my breath. Trinity collected keys to all sorts of outlandish places, and there was something magical that he did with them, although I didn't know what yet. He was also a Mesmer, and could entrance humans with his suggestions. While his glamour didn't work on me, it didn't go unnoticed. I did find him mesmerizing and hypnotic, though, and I liked being around him.

"What do you say? One journey tonight. And then I'll tell you my secret—possibly." He grinned, tilting his head in a dare.

I let out an exasperated sigh but nodded. "All right. One journey, in exchange for one secret."

"Possibly." Trinity tossed a fifty-dollar bill on the table, then motioned for me to join him as he sauntered out of the door.

"ARE you going to tell me your secret?" I asked as I drove in the direction he wanted to go. We were headed for the Worchester District, the most haunted area of Seattle. I wasn't thrilled about the idea of running into more spirits, but if we did, we did.

"Oh no, you get your secret when we've finished our journey."

"So, does your new key lead to a mausoleum? A grave?"

Trinity shook his head. "Nope, it's not actually a new key. But I did discover a new secret, and I think you'll like it. You'll just have to wait and see." He paused for a moment, then added, "How is Kipa doing? How are you two doing?"

I pressed my lips together for a moment. As tired as I was of people asking me that, I felt like I could talk to Trinity. He didn't judge, just listened. I couldn't even talk to Llew about my relationship right now, because Llew was fixated on the idea that if I just asked for therapy, everything would be all right.

"Kipa's all right. We need to make this quick because I'm meeting him at nine back at my house. And I've broken too many promises lately to stand him up again tonight." I sighed, pausing. Finally, I added, "The truth is that I'm both afraid I'll lose Kipa, and I'm afraid he'll stay. Because if he stays, he just might realize how messed up I am. I don't want him to know how badly this fucked up my mind. He's worried enough as it is."

"We're almost there. Traffic's light tonight." Trinity

leaned back in his seat, sliding his hands behind his head. "What does Kipa think about our friendship?"

I glanced at Trinity, then back at the road. "I think he's jealous. I told him he has nothing to worry about, that you and I have no romantic interest in each other. I trust I'm right on that, aren't I?" Trinity and I had never really discussed our sudden friendship. But I wanted to make sure that he was on the same page I was.

"Don't worry," he said. "I'm not going to try to jump your bones. Not that you aren't attractive, but right now, I'm not particularly interested in getting involved with anybody. I don't fuck my friends because I don't want to lose them and inevitably, when I sleep with a woman, she always seems to want more than I have to offer." He pointed to a side street. "Over there."

The Worchester District of Seattle was old and falling-down decrepit. Spirits gathered here, especially in some of the older buildings that had housed the mentally ill at a time when mental illness was treated as a dirty secret, and some of the private boarding schools for delinquents that had been shut down when their unorthodox punishments were brought to light.

I parked at the end of Broadfen Avenue near a sign that read "Dead End Street." As we locked the car and began to walk down the road, I realized that the entire street seemed to be abandoned. The road was lined with apartments on either side, all of them dilapidated and empty. The buildings were silent and dark, their court-yards overgrown.

The buildings to our left and right had once been apart-ment buildings—two long rows of them on either side. They were brownstone brick, and they bore fading signs that read "Broadfen Townhouses." The windows were broken from people throwing stones, and the doors were boarded up with rotting sheets of plywood. Broadfen was a short street, and up ahead, I could see that it ended at a chain-link fence.

As we approached the fence, I could see that beyond the Broadfen brownstones on either side, there were buildings that looked to be part of some complex. When I squinted, I could see a fading sign on the end of the one on the right that read "UCHV—Building B." Another building kitty-corner to the left of the garden looked similar. Obviously, we had found some sort of complex. But that wasn't what caught my attention. No, what drew my focus was what lay beyond the chain-link fence.

There was a garden there, between the two long buildings, spreading out in a square like a courtyard. On the other side of the garden I could barely see—through the tangle of trees and foliage—another building that ran lengthwise to the garden square.

"What is this place?" I asked.

"I'm not sure. I just discovered it yesterday. Let's explore the garden!"

The fence was low, about three feet high. To the left, right before the fence, was a pile of broken concrete that littered the road. There was no gate.

Trinity leaped over the fence with no problem. He turned as I clambered up to the top of the concrete debris. He held out his hand, steadying me as I cautiously placed my left foot on the fence. Trinity caught my other hand as I balanced on the metal rail before swinging down to the other side. Letting go, he held his finger to his lips and we crept into the overgrown garden.

I glanced around. The chain link ran the entire perimeter of the garden, which was sandwiched between the four buildings—the one in back of us belonging to the Broadfen brownstones.

Square, the lot was about twice the size of my backyard. Even from where we were, I could see vining maple and ivy growing up the walls of the buildings. In the garden proper, there was a riot of flowers and shrubs, along with a giant maple tree, several lilacs, and knee-deep grass and ferns that blanketed the ground. A riot of wild roses and foxglove poked out of the knee-high grass. The lilacs were done and gone, but the scent of the roses filled the air, intoxicating me, their blossoms were so fragrant. In the center of the garden was a stone bench, barely visible in the thick grass and ferns that covered the ground.

"How did you find this place?" I asked, looking around, delighted. It was like a hidden oasis in the middle of a dismal part of the city.

"I like to take long walks. I go on treasure quests to discover the hidden wild places of Seattle. You need to be cautious—I've seen a few nixienacks around here, but they tend to come out more during the day rather than in the evening." Trinity led me over to the bench. "Have a seat."

I sat down, trying to relax as I leaned back and drew a deep breath. Trinity was kneeling nearby, sorting through a pile of discarded objects. I closed my eyes, thinking that I should be relaxing given the beauty of the garden, but instead, I felt a dark pall looming over my shoulder. I turned toward the building on the opposite side, staring at it.

The buildings that surrounded the garden were long silent, abandoned like so many places in the Worchester District. But even though the living had left them behind, I could feel the dead moving inside. There were throngs of them here, crowding the spiritual highways.

I watched the building closely. It was gloomy, large and taciturn, and the longer I looked at it, the more nervous it made me. I frowned, staring at one of the upper windows that overlooked the garden. There was somebody watching me, and it made me uncomfortable.

"What was that building used for?" I asked.

Trinity glanced up from the debris pile. "I think it was an infirmary or something. I'm not sure, though. Why?"

"There's something there. I mean, there are ghosts all over the place around here, but there's some spirit in that building that feels…trapped? I want to say trapped." I worried my lip, both wanting to go explore, and yet being afraid to do so.

"It's not Pandora, is it? Trying to charm you again?" Trinity was standing now, pushing his jacket back to reveal a wicked-looking blade strapped to his belt.

I shook my head. "I don't think so. I think someone in there might need my help."

At that moment, a piercing shriek raced through the astral, almost knocking me over with its fear. I jumped back, trying to catch my breath. There was a spirit in trouble, and the sound of her terror rang in my head.

Trinity's eyes widened. "I heard it too." He paused, then glanced at his phone. "Come on, we should leave. You need to get home."

"But I want to check it out—" I started to say, then stopped as Trinity pushed me toward the chain-link gate.

"I shouldn't have brought you here," he said. "I just thought you'd like the garden."

I protested again that I *did* like the garden, and that I thought we should explore the building, but Trinity wouldn't hear of it. He hustled me back over the fence and toward my car, and before I could say a word, we were on the way back to the Eastside. I wanted to ask him more about the building, but I could sense that he truly regretted taking me there and I knew I wouldn't get a clear answer. I knew, too, that I wouldn't get an answer to my question about his secret, so I let both thoughts drop as I focused on driving. But my mind was back in the secret garden, back with the wandering ghosts, and I knew that I'd return.

CHAPTER FOUR

I MADE IT HOME SHORTLY BEFORE KIPA WAS DUE TO ARRIVE. Trinity headed off into the evening on foot, even though I offered to drop him somewhere. He disappeared into UnderLake Park and I watched him go, wondering where he lived. He still hadn't told me, and every time I asked, he just shrugged and changed the subject.

Raj was waiting for me, and I curled up with him on the sofa. "Kipa's coming over. Raj likes Kipa, right?"

Raj wiggled his butt, looking a lot like a happy rottweiler. He walked much like an orangutan, on his back feet and his knuckles. But up close, it was obvious he was a gargoyle, with leathery gray skin, sans wings. The faint scars on his back were a grim reminder of where the demon who had first owned him had cut his wings off. I had managed to find someone to cast a memory loss spell on him, so he'd never remember either the pain or the loss.

"Raj loves Kipa." He glanced over his shoulder at the TV. "Raven take Raj for a walk in the park?"

I sighed. We hadn't gone for a walk in a while. Kipa had taken Raj out to let him wander around. But I had been remiss, and I felt bad about it. Every time I tried to take him out to the park, I would get to the edge of the trailhead and stop, wondering who or what I would find inside the borders, and then I'd turn back and take him on a quick walk around the block.

"Well, maybe Kipa and Raven can take Raj for a walk tonight. Would Raj like that?" With Kipa alongside of us, I wouldn't feel so spooked.

"Raj would like that. Very much." He looked so excited that I knew I had to keep my word.

Ten minutes later, Kipa knocked at the door.

I opened it, frowning. "Why didn't you use your key?" Kipa had a key, and he knew he had the run of my place.

He looked a little uncomfortable. "I wasn't sure whether you wanted me to knock or not. I didn't want to spook you." Even as he said it, I knew that what he meant was that he didn't want to piss me off.

"I'm sorry," I said, trying to find the words to smooth everything over. I stared at him for a moment, looking at those full lips and warm brown eyes, and I suddenly burst into tears, throwing my arms around his waist and resting my head on his shoulder. "I don't mean to be so difficult. I really don't. I'm just having a lot of trouble lately and I don't know what to say or do. Nothing feels right anymore."

Kipa slowly kissed the top of my head, then gently unwound me, moving me back so he could gaze into my eyes. "Raven, we really need to talk about this. We need to get you some help. There's no shame in needing to talk to somebody about something as horrific as what you went through."

I wiped my eyes, knowing that I had to face the "talk" sometime, so it might as well be now. "Yeah, I know. Why don't we take Raj for a walk in the park and we can talk as we go?"

Kipa nodded. "I'd like that very much."

I put on Raj's harness and fastened his leash to it, then changed my shoes for ones I could run in easily. As I set the alarm and made sure the wards were still strong, Kipa and Raj waited for me down in the driveway. I shut the door, locking it soundly, and slid the keys in my pocket. We headed over to the trailhead, and I took a deep breath as I stared at the opening. UnderLake Park never scared me before, not even when Ulstair was found dead there. Now, it loomed like a threatening cloud. I glanced over at Kipa.

"Are you sure you want to do this?" he asked me.

I nodded. "I have to. I can't just sit here and let fear rule my life. I can't let it lock me away behind my front door, afraid to go out anywhere." Summoning up my courage, I set foot on the trail and we headed in.

UNDERLAKE PARK SPRAWLED for five hundred acres, full of trails and waterfront property. A massive thicket of trees and meadows, the park had a sinister history. At one point most of the acreage had belonged to a group of monks who had vanished over the years.

The monastery, fully haunted with both spirits and memories, stood solemn and looming shortly beyond the front entrance, but few ever went near it because it was said that some of the monks had returned, unable to rest because of sins they had committed during life.

Fifty acres of the park had been donated by the Castle family. Their estate head once ruled over a meticulously groomed set of gardens, and they had been an influential family until the owners were brutally murdered. At least, that's what police thought happened to them.

Their bodies had never been found, but so much blood had been left at the scene of what seemed like a psycho-crazed slaughter that doctors said whoever the victims had been, they couldn't have survived such a bloodletting. At least two people had been murdered, and it was just assumed that it was John and Vera Castle. Their daughter donated the land to the city, unable to face living there once her parents disappeared.

Like most of the parks in the Seattle area, UnderLake Park was heavily wooded, with deep ravines gouging the surface. Trails crisscrossed the park, jogging trails, walking trails, and even a few minor hiking trails that provided a good workout. Ulstair, my late fiancé, had been caught by a serial killer and murdered in the woods not far from my home. That was when I had met Herne and Ember, and the Wild Hunt. They had helped me track down the killer, and I rested easily because, at the last moment, I had taken matters into my own hands. That particular killer would never walk the world again. After I had dispatched him, I had secretly done a spell binding his spirit away from the physical plane forever. And I had said good-bye to my love, letting him fade into history.

Kipa and I set out on one of the gentler graded walking trails. Raj happily strained at the leash, wanting to look at anything and everything. We came to a picnic table in a clearing, and I motioned to it. "Why don't we let Raj off leash for a while? We can sit and talk." I turned to Raj. "If Raven lets Raj off Raj's leash, will Raj promise not to run off? Does Raj promise to stay within sight?"

Raj gave me a puppy-dog look, then shrugged and giggled. "Raj promises. Raj won't go out of sight."

I leaned down and let him off the leash. He might remind me of a dog, but he wasn't one, and he wouldn't just run up to strangers and jump all over them. Nor did he chase other creatures unless I gave him the go-ahead. But he liked to wander around and play in the shrubs, and poke around the trunks of the trees.

Kipa and I sat down at the picnic table, where we could keep an eye on Raj.

"Sometimes lately I feel like I've been going crazy," I said, finally meeting his gaze. He said nothing, letting me continue to speak without interruption. "I've been having flashbacks. I'll be fine one minute, and then something will trigger a flashback and I'll be back in that cavern, where she's pulling off my nails and pulling out my teeth. And I remember how helpless I felt, and how I was so certain I would never walk out of that cave alive." I pressed my lips together, shaking my head. "What I hate is the randomness of it. How I'll be doing something normal —cleaning out the ferrets' cage or putting away dishes or something like that, and the next minute I'm there on her table again. And what I hate most is that *I'm* the one who put myself in danger. *I* gave her a ride home that night, *I* befriended her at the club, and *I* didn't think twice about letting her in my car because we had talked for a couple hours. I'm afraid that I've lost my sense of self-preservation. As I open up more to people and make new friends, I let down my guard. And this time, it almost killed me. What if that happens again? How can I ever open myself to anybody again without knowing it won't happen again?"

Kipa stretched out his hands, opening them up to me. "Raven, it wasn't your fault. So you let down your guard? You were just trying to help someone that you thought was caught in a predicament. You were being a good person. We shouldn't have to live in a world where we're constantly wondering if someone's going to kill us. We shouldn't have to pause when we meet someone because we don't know if they're going to turn out to be a psycho. *You're* not the one with the problem."

I took his hands in mine, squeezing hard. "The world has always been like this. And it probably will always be like this. But I've changed. My mother didn't like the fact that I wanted to hang around humans so much, that I'm an Exosan. She warned me and she cautioned my father when she realized that I liked people more than she thought appropriate. Now I understand why." I worried my lip as I looked up to meet his gaze. The warmth in his eyes flooded my heart, making me feel even more torn.

"That's why you've backed away, isn't it? You're afraid we'll get too close, and being close means being vulnerable."

I nodded, tears streaking down my cheek. "I care about you more than I've ever cared about anybody except for Ulstair and Raj. But I loved Ulstair and he died. And I almost died in the same way. I don't understand what's going on."

Kipa paused. "For one thing, no, for most people it's

not normal to run into two serial killers in a lifetime. But think about it. You're friends with Herne and Ember, and their business specializes with murderers and monsters and things that go bump in the night. And then, you're a bone witch, so of course you're steeped in the world of spirits. You're bound to find yourself dealing with people who've been murdered."

"Good point," I said, letting his words sink in.

"You live in a shadow world, Raven. There's no mysterious curse on your head, there's no hex binding you to a life filled with the Ted Bundys of the world. Your world surrounds death and ghosts, and where there's death, there will be murder and accidents and terrible things that caused people to lose their lives." He paused, looking frustrated. "I don't know if I'm saying this the best way, or if I'm making any sense."

He wouldn't let go of my hands, keeping me focused on him. I took a few deep breaths, thinking about what he said.

"Yeah, I do see that. I didn't think about it in those terms," I said.

"At the core of it, though, I think you're afraid. Pandora caught you and had you under her control. Until then, you had tremendous self-confidence. Unfortunately, the gods are stronger than the Ante-Fae. There's always going to be someone stronger than you, and there's always going to be someone weaker. Even among the gods, we have to face that. We may not be mortal, but we aren't all-powerful. Right now, Annwn is buzzing as the gods try to figure out how to deal with Typhon. All of us together aren't as powerful as he is. And Mielikki's Arrow, and Odin's Chase, and Diana's

Hounds, and dozens of other organizations and groups in the divine community are facing the same thing. Typhon is one of the ancient Titans. He's the Father of Dragons. Together, the gods can't defeat him. Not yet. And even then, we'll only be able to drive him back into stasis. He's one of the Immortals. So you see, there's *always* somebody bigger and badder. And that's scary when you've run into them and seen firsthand what they can—and will—do."

I glanced to the side, making sure Raj was still within sight. Then, I slowly turned back to Kipa. "A question. The gods are immortal, so doesn't that give you some peace of mind? I mean, I know I might as well be immortal compared to a human, but... When I was lying there on that table I felt my life slipping away. And I realized that I *can* and *will* die someday. And it was a shock."

He thought about it for a moment, then shook his head. "I think it goes beyond that. I think you've always understood your mortality. But isn't it possible that a deeper fear crept in—the fear and realization that you had no control? That somebody had power over you? As long as I've known you, you've never let anyone dictate what you do, what you wear, who you choose as friends. The moment that Pandora captured you, she stripped all of your autonomy away, and you were entirely in her power. You were totally vulnerable."

I stared at him, feeling short of breath. The panic rose, coursing through my veins. Everything began to spin as the world spiraled out from beneath my feet. Even though we were outside, I felt as though everything was closing in. I pulled my hands away from Kipa, stumbling over the bench as I tried to back away.

"No, I don't want to think about it. I don't want to remember!"

I grabbed the sides of my head, falling to my knees as the world spun around me.

I was back in the cavern with Pandora standing over me and her laugh echoed from every side of the chamber. I began to whimper as I realized she'd stripped away my ability to withstand pain. And I heard myself screaming, begging my mother to help me, begging my father to rescue me. And then I was begging for Kipa to save me, but no one was there. No one except for Pandora and me, locked in a dark little world where she could do anything she wanted and there was nothing I could do to stop her.

"Raven! Raven, are you all right? Raven, speak to me!"

Kipa's voice echoed through the fog in my head, cutting through the mist like a lifeline. I grabbed hold of it, and he pulled me out.

Terrified, I leaned into his embrace as he held me, murmuring gently.

"Raven? Is Raven okay?" Raj's voice echoed and I opened my eyes to find him leaning against me. I turned, throwing my arms around his neck, leaning my head against his back as I sobbed. I couldn't talk, couldn't even think, but at least I could smell the grass and the trees around me, and I was breathing freely again.

"Oh my love, I'm so sorry." Kipa's voice was gentle, as he stroked the hair back from my face. "I didn't mean to trigger you."

"I know you didn't. I know you were just trying to help."

I could barely catch my voice, but as I glanced up at him I saw the worry and the love in his eyes and even though we hadn't said those words, I could feel that he cared about me, and that he loved me.

"I'm sorry. Maybe you're right, maybe it's time I talked to someone about this. I can't believe she did this to me," I said, still crying angry tears. "I hate that she lives in my head. It would be different if we had been able to kill her. She'd be gone. But she's still out there."

"I know, and we'll do everything we can to make sure she never comes back. Herne suggested that Ferosyn could find you a therapist." He said the latter gingerly, as though I were going to bite his head off. I didn't blame him. I had done a lot of biting lately.

I kissed Raj again, then brushed my hands over my eyes, trying to wipe away the tears. "Yeah. Would you call him for me? Ask him if he could contact Ferosyn? I know that he helped Rafé after his ordeal."

"And you didn't look down on Rafé for asking for help, did you?" Kipa extended his hand, helping me stand. Raj stuck close to my feet, keeping just out of the way.

I shook my head. "No, in fact I suggested he ask for help. I guess I just never thought I would be in the position to need to do the same." I paused, then turned to Kipa. "Trinity is just a friend. Please don't feel insecure or jealous. I don't want to push you away, even though I know that I've been hard to live with the past few weeks. I want you in my life."

Kipa stared at me for a moment, and I wasn't sure what he was going to say. Part of me was afraid that it was too late, that I had been too difficult to handle.

But when he spoke, his voice was soft—not angry. "When Herne and I were looking for you, I told him something. I was going to tell you when we found you, but everything was so mixed up and you were so hurt. So I put it on the back burner, hoping for the right time. I think *now* is that time."

A chill raced across my heart. Barely able to breathe, I asked, "What is it?"

"I love you, Raven. I loved you for a while now, but I thought it was too early to say so."

I closed my eyes, reeling with the words. "You aren't going to leave me? I haven't driven you away?"

He shook his head, a smile widening across his face. "No, babe. I don't promise forever, I don't think any of the gods or the Ante-Fae can do that. But I'm here, and I love you, and I'll stay as long as you want me."

With those words, he broke through the wall and I burst into tears again, crying for the pain I had endured, crying for Pandora's other victims, crying for the darkness the world was facing, and crying because I had lost my heart to a god and I knew that I couldn't pretend otherwise anymore.

"I love you too, Kipa."

And with that, we walked back to the house and shut out the night, safely behind locked doors.

CHAPTER FIVE

I WOKE UP THE NEXT MORNING, SQUINTING AS SUNLIGHT filtered between the drapes. I glanced over my shoulder to see Kipa snoring away, the covers half-sprawled over his torso. We hadn't made love, but that was okay. It was going to take me a while to get back in the groove, and I was grateful that he hadn't pushed me. I could tell he was more than ready—his cock was peeking out from behind the covers, fully erect and ready—but last night he had simply given me a long back massage, not pushing and not trying to rush me. Then he brought me pizza and milk in bed, and rubbed my feet while I ate. I slept better than I had in weeks.

I yawned and stretched. The exhaustion I had felt every morning since I had gotten home from Annwn seemed to have lifted. I knew it was too good to last, at least for now, but it was a welcome respite. Heading over to the window, I opened the sash, leaning on the sill as the fresh breeze wafted through. A nice tall fence separated me from the neighbors, so they couldn't see in, and the breeze felt good against my naked body.

"Good morning," Kipa said.

I turned around, smiling as he pushed himself up against the headboard so he was sitting up. I opened the door and Raj came in, lumbering over to crawl on the bed. Kipa rubbed him on the back, and Raj let out a little grunt of enjoyment. He liked being petted, even though the leathery skin was about as far from fur as you could get.

"I need to take a shower and then tend to the ferrets." I turned to Kipa. "Would you feed Raj and start breakfast for us?"

He nodded. "Sure thing. Angel taught me how to make French toast the other day. Would you like that?"

"That sounds good, and bacon. *Lots* of bacon." I looked at Raj. "And don't you try to wheedle Kipa into giving you cat food this morning. I think you need something a bit more nutritious." It wasn't that cat food was bad for him; but it was an expensive treat and I had been giving it to him to make up for feeling emotionally distant. While I felt good, it was time to start breaking some bad habits I'd let myself fall into. "If you'd make Raj some oatmeal and some eggs, that would be good. Meanwhile, I'm going to get my ass in the shower and have a good wash."

As I padded into the bathroom, I heard Kipa getting up and dressing. I closed the door softly behind me, staring at myself in the mirror.

The tattoos covering my body—well, they were actually birthmarks, although they *looked* like tattoos—seemed more vivid than they had been in weeks. When I was feeling subpar, they seemed to mute, though they never left me entirely. Today, they seemed to sparkle more.

The patterns were from my parents. The wings swirling on my back were a mark that my mother was one of the Bean Sidhe—the Queen, actually. Some of the others that worked their way down my arms and across my chest and torso I had inherited from my father, the Black Dog of Hanging Hills. Curikan was his name.

I shook my hair. It now reached to my lower back and I was trying to decide whether to have a few inches cut off or not. It was black with purple streaks that run through it—another natural coloration.

I headed to the shower, turning the water to a pleasantly warm setting. As I slipped in under the spray, I caught my breath and closed my eyes as I relaxed. I lathered up, suddenly realizing that I was aroused as I brushed the loofah over my nipples. I hadn't felt sexual in weeks, either. I thought about calling Kipa in, but then decided that I didn't want to start something I might not be able to finish. I didn't want to disappoint him, or myself. I turned the water to cold, blasting myself with an icy rinse, and stepped out of the stall.

I finished washing my hair, then quickly dried off. As I pulled out my blow dryer, I couldn't get my mind off the spirit who had screamed for help. My normal inclination would be to check out the situation and help if I could. And right there, I decided that I wouldn't let my fear stop me from doing the right thing. I made a decision to go check out the building and see what I could find out. Llew was right. I couldn't lock myself away forever. It was time to ask for help and reclaim my life. But I'd learned my lesson. Never trust strangers, and don't make friends so fast.

I dressed and headed for the ferrets' room.

Gordon and Templeton were still snoozing, but Elise was awake and waiting for me. They weren't really ferrets —or rather they *were*, but they were more than ferrets. I had discovered three spirits cursed and trapped in a tree up on Mount Rainier years before, and in trying to free them, I had ended up turning them into ferrets. Now, they were trapped in their ferret bodies, living far beyond the average lifespan of the creatures.

Gordon, pure white and slinky, had practically turned into a ferret, and Templeton, all black, was headed that way, though he was still able to resist the temptation to give in and let the animal nature take over. But Elise, who was sable brown and lovely, had managed to keep her sense of self. She stood up to the cage as I came in, her nose moving a mile a minute.

"Good morning, Elise. How are you doing?" I hadn't spent much time with them the past few weeks, though I always made sure their cages were cleaned and they were taken care of.

Elise stared at me for a moment, then—as I unlocked the cage door so they could have a run around the room— she cocked her head.

I was wondering the same thing. How are you, Raven? I'm not quite sure what happened, but you've been acting distant lately, and nervous.

Elise's thoughts came through quite clearly to me. I wasn't sure how we managed to communicate, but I just appreciated that we could. I pressed my lips together for a moment, then sat at the table, picking her up so she could sit on my lap. Although Elise remembered her days when she had been alive, she still liked to be petted and groomed, like most pets.

"I know, and I'm sorry. I haven't really wanted to talk about everything that's happened. I had... I was..." I paused, not wanting to distress her. But she could tell when I was covering up something, and she had become a good friend over the years. I felt I owed her the truth.

"I was caught by an emissary for Typhon. Remember, I told you about him?"

Yes, the Father of Dragons.

"That's right. He's broken out of his slumber and he's hiding somewhere in the Phantom Kingdom right now. But he's sent emissaries to pave the way, and he's also unlocked the gates for his children to return. So in December, I ended up being captured by one of his emissaries. Remember when I was gone for a couple weeks?"

Yes, Kipa took care of us during that time.

"Right. I was healing up over in Annwn. Pandora, Zeus's daughter, is working for Typhon and she caught me. I was tortured and almost didn't make it. I've been having flashbacks since then. I really haven't been myself. But I am going to talk to Herne's friend Ferosyn, the healer who patched me up, and see if he can recommend a good therapist. I seem to be having trouble getting over some of the trauma." I paused, wondering how much to tell her. Elise was a gentle soul, though resilient, and while I counted her a friend, I didn't like wounding her sensitive nature.

Oh Raven, I'm so sorry. I knew something was wrong, but I had no clue it was anything like that. Is there anything we can do? I know we're just ferrets now, but...you can always talk to me if you need to. Elise pressed her front paws against my chest, staring into my face. She nuzzled me with a soft *chook-chook.*

"Thank you, Elise. You're sweet and I'm grateful for the offer, but I don't want to burden you. Seeing a therapist will help more than anything." Actually, what would help more than anything was to see Pandora dead, but she was a goddess and that wasn't possible. Next best thing? Mental health therapy.

I stroked her back, smiling as she wriggled in delight. I had promised the ferrets I would search for a curse-breaker to the hex that bound them in ferret form, but I had come up empty time and again. I was starting to think we'd never find anything to help. If that was the case, then eventually even Elise would lose herself into her ferret nature, and they'd live out their days in the quiet world of being pets, returning to the spirits of their former selves after their bodies gave out. But at least they weren't trapped in a tree anymore.

Elise jumped down after a bit and I cleaned out their cage, changing their bedding and filling their food and water bowls. After I finished and they were tired from running around, I returned them to the cage and gently locked the door. I leaned against the metal frame, staring at them.

Thank you for sitting with us. Elise glanced at me. *Remember, if I can help in any way...*

"I'll remember. Thank you for caring." I opened the window a crack to let some fresh air in, then washed my hands in the adjoining bathroom and headed to the kitchen where Kipa was making breakfast.

KIPA HAD breakfast ready when I entered the dining room.

French toast dusted with powdered sugar, scrambled eggs, bacon, lattes with thick heads of foam, and a platter of grapes and strawberries. I slid into my chair and forked thick slices of the bread onto my plate, spreading butter on them and then dousing them with syrup. I was the kind of woman who preferred some pancakes or waffles with my syrup, as opposed to some syrup on my pancakes or waffles. The bread was just a vehicle to support the toppings.

Kipa had fed Raj, who was happily munching away in the corner. Raj glanced over his shoulder at me, spitting food all over the floor as he said "Good morning" before going back to breakfast.

"You didn't give him cat food, did you?"

"I did not. Turns out if you mix a little maple syrup in the oatmeal, he loves it. Go figure."

Kipa was dressed in a light green V-neck sweater, the sleeves shoved up to his elbows, and a pair of black leather jeans. He had on a silver belt buckle in the shape of a wolf's head, and his hair was pulled back into a pony-tail. Gorgeous, with golden skin and a dolphin bite piercing in his lip, Kipa also had the darkest brown eyes I had ever seen. He was magnetically handsome, yet a play-ful, caring energy filled his aura.

"Well, that's good to know." I set to my breakfast, wondering whether I should bring up our sex life—or lack of one. I didn't want Kipa to think I'd gone cold on him. He probably understood, but given our discussion the night before, it made sense to open up all the way on the changes that had happened lately.

"Hey, about our sex life…" I licked syrup off my finger and sat back, frowning.

"You're not feeling all too safe letting down your guard right now?" He gave me that look that told me he already knew what I was going to say.

I nodded. "I just don't want you to think that I'm not interested in you."

"Don't worry. That part of our relationship will fall back into place once you process all this baggage Pandora dumped in your lap." He finished off a slice of the French toast and added, "Just keep me up to date on where you're at. I don't want to push you, or rush you, so it's on your timetable. I'll be waiting when you're ready again." After a pause, he asked, "What are you going to do today?"

I wiped my hands on my napkin. "I'm going to examine a building that I ran across last night. It's abandoned, and I think it has a couple of trapped spirits in it." I glanced across the table at him.

Kipa slowly stretched, yawning. Then, in a casual way that was anything but casual, he asked, "Want me to go with you?"

I shook my head. "No, that's not necessary. Don't you have a busy day ahead? I thought Ember said that today they're going to be reconnoitering some space over on Bainbridge and they wanted you to go along."

"Nope. That's not for another couple weeks, and yes, I do have to go. But today I'm free." He paused, eyeing me carefully. "Are you *sure* you don't want me to come along with you?"

I thought about it for a moment. Having Kipa along would set me at ease, but I was tired of being afraid. I wanted to feel the way I used to—relentless, capable, sure of myself. And he would try to cushion the blows, which would make me less effective.

"No, I think I want to do this myself. But if you're up to it, Raj could use a real run in the park. We didn't get very far yesterday, thanks to me." I stared at Raj glumly, feeling guilty.

"I can do that. But promise you'll text me if anything happens? Even if *nothing* happens?" He leaned forward. "I can't help worrying about you. I've never known anybody quite like you, Raven. And I know that I've got a bad track record, but now…you mean more to me than anybody I've known in…well…centuries."

I slowly reached across the table and took his hands. "You know who my last important relationship was with. I know from Ember that you and Herne's ex…well…"

"You mean Nya, his fiancée? I knew this would come up some time." He ducked his head, looking embarrassed. "I admit, at the time I was an asshole and I'm not proud of what I did. At that time, I didn't give a fuck about anybody else. Nya was pretty, and Herne was so full of himself. Ember doesn't know how much of a fuckup he could be and I'm not going to tell her, but there were things he did that weren't any better than the crap I pulled."

I laughed. "I believe you. I like Herne but with as long as he's lived, there have got to be some situations he's really screwed up. So, tell me…was Nya the woman you last fell for?"

He leaned back in his chair. "No, actually. I'm going to tell you something I've never told anyone, especially Herne. And I don't want him knowing. The fact is, I wasn't that interested in Nya until she came onto me. *She's* the one who seduced me. Yes, I could have refused but I didn't. But...*I* didn't initiate the encounter. Nya was bored and I was a wild child."

"Then you weren't out to take her away from Herne?"

"Gods no," he said. "She was a ditz." He paused, then squeezed my hand. "No, the last woman I truly loved was from around three hundred and fifty years ago."

"Woman...she wasn't a goddess?"

He shook his head. "Actually, Venla was human. I lived with her from the day we met—she was about twenty—until the day she died, sixty-four years later. I took care of her. I loved her. I held her when she was dying, and I buried her. And before you ask, no, we didn't have any children. She couldn't have any. She had been beaten when she was young and the beating injured her uterus. Her stepfather beat her for refusing him, then cast her out from her family. I found her in the woods one day, when she was out hunting for dinner." He closed his eyes. "Herne never knew about her. Nobody did. I just vanished for that time period, and after I left the home we had built together, I never told anyone about Venla. Not until now."

I stood, circling the table till I was standing beside him. "You gave your heart to her."

"Yes, I did. And she's held it all these years. Until I met you." He looked up at me, his dark eyes flashing. "I've slept with a lot of women since then, but none of them reminded me of Venla. And you don't, either, not in the way that you might think. But she was a rebel, and strong-willed, and so are you. She never let me forget that I had been *invited* into her life, not the other way around. She made me a better man while I was with her. And Raven, you make me a better man now."

I pressed against him as he draped his arm around my

hips. "Never be afraid to talk about her, please. I *want* you to remember her. I want you to not be afraid to still love her, like I will always love Ulstair. I know that the love you have for me isn't any the lesser because she held your heart first." I leaned down and kissed him.

His expression crumpled, and a tear trickled down his cheek. "Thank you. I've never talked about Venla because I didn't want to remember losing her. And if I had told Herne about her, well, at one time—not now, but back then—he would have laughed at me and called me a liar."

I pressed my lips against the tear gliding down his cheek, gently sucking the droplet between my lips. "You taste like the ocean," I whispered.

He pulled me onto his lap, his lips meeting mine in a hungry, desperate crush. I kissed him back, and I could feel his urgency build. I wanted him, and I knew he needed me. He needed to remind himself that he was still alive, even though Venla was gone. He needed reassurance and passion and all those wonderful things that went into making up a relationship.

"Take me into the bedroom," I whispered.

"Are you sure?"

I kissed him again. "I'm sure."

So Kipa lifted me up and carried me into the bedroom, and I was able to let down my guard. He loved me, long and passionately, and yet as gentle as the morning breeze that drifted over us from the open window. And when I came, he kissed me again, and he kept kissing me as we lingered in the bed until Raj knocked on the door to ask for a snack.

CHAPTER SIX

Kipa offered to do the grocery shopping while I headed out to check on the haunted building. I felt better than I had in quite a while, and my relationship didn't feel like it was on such shaky ground.

The drive over the bridge to Seattle went smoothly. It was late enough that rush-hour traffic had backed off, but not so late that the noon rush had begun. I pulled up Broadfen on the GPS and when I got there, had no problem finding a parking space on the cross street.

The walk down the side street seemed less ominous during the daylight, and the fact that the sky was clear and the temperature was almost seventy-five degrees lent a surreal brilliance to everything. The streeps were out of their makeshift homes, out on the main streets panhandling for money, and there were no shoppers along the route. In fact, Broadfen itself was empty when I turned onto it. While I knew I could handle myself in most cases, some of the streeps could be pretty violent if they were jacked up on crackalaine. It was one of those drugs like PCP that increased strength as well as psychosis.

The Broadfen brownstones were silent, though I had no doubt some of the streeps had found their way in to use them for cover from the weather. Squatters were common in the desolate areas of the city. I saw a few rats scrambling on the sidewalk and avoided them. While there weren't any active shops along the street, if there were streeps squatting in the buildings, there would be refuse and debris. On the surface, Seattle didn't seem to have a lot of vermin, but beneath the glamour of the Emerald City, the seedy neighborhoods and streeps and back-alley rodents were the constant underpinnings.

I shaded my eyes, wishing I had brought my sunglasses. The sun was glinting down, splashing across one side of the buildings next to me. I crossed to the other side, welcoming the shadow. It wasn't that I didn't like the sun, but right now it made me feel too exposed.

In fact, the juxtaposition almost confused me. Here we were, facing an invasion by the Father of Dragons and his spawn, facing an upsurge of ghosts and spirits and all the undead who walked in Typhon's shadow, and yet the sun was shining so brightly that it felt like there could be no hidden agenda, no silent war being waged on the world.

While I didn't have many friends who were necro-mancers, I knew enough of them to know they were being run ragged. In fact, Lane, one of the few friends I had actually made on my ill-fated visit to the Spooks group, had called me a week ago to warn me that the graveyards were quickly becoming unsafe for humans. And seeing that she was a powerful necromancer, her warning came with a serious punch behind it.

But I'm not going to a graveyard, and it's not nighttime. I'm in the middle of the city, downtown, and it's broad daylight.

I came to the chain-link fence that Trinity and I had climbed over. The previous night I had scrambled over thanks to the debris pile, but it was shaky, so I glanced around, figuring how to best clear the fence. The pile of broken bricks and concrete contained enough pieces small enough for me to lift, so I managed to create a stairstep-type pile next to the fence. It wasn't entirely steady, but since the fencing was only three feet high, all I needed was a step up so I could swing over without catching my skirts on it.

As I dropped to the other side, I found myself back in the secret garden.

During the day, the garden was a cacophony of color, brilliant and beautiful, and the heady scent of the flowers under the sun made my head swim. I slowly walked over to the bench and sat down, turning so that I could look at the building in which I had sensed the trapped spirit.

What had all these buildings been when they were in use?

Biting my lip, I stood up and trundled my way through the deep grass, brushing away spiders and bugs until I was standing at the fence again, facing the building to the right. It was a few hundred feet outside the chain link. A large sign on the front was faded, but I could still read it: UCHV—Building B, the same thing that was on the sign on the end of the building.

The doors and windows were boarded over, but from where I stood it looked like it had once been an apartment building of some sort, but more utilitarian than the Broadfen brownstones. This looked more clinical.

I frowned, glancing back across the garden. The building on the other side looked just as dilapidated, and it also looked empty. I squinted, trying to see if there was a sign over the door, and then finally caught sight of it. This one read UCHV—Building A.

Okay, so these two buildings went together, and that must mean the one at the end of the garden belonged to whatever complex this had been. I followed the chain-link fence to the end, then turned left and followed it till I was standing in the middle of the garden, at an actual gate. The building directly in front of me had a slightly different look than buildings A and B, but it had the same feel and style to it. They had definitely been built by the same developer.

The gate was rusty, but I was able to open it. I stepped through, ducking through the natural arch created by a tangle of two maple trees that flanked the gate, pushing past the knee-high grass that had overgrown the entire area. There was a bench on the other side, facing the third building. And then, a thought occurred to me. I brushed away a thick layer of debris on the bench and sat down, pulling out my phone. Bringing up my Maps app, I scrolled through until I found my location. As I expanded the screen, a description window came up. The three buildings made up what had once been the United Coalition's Home for Wounded Veterans.

A home for soldiers.

But I had the feeling there was a lot more to this place than met the eye, so I brought up a browser and typed the name into the search bar. Sure enough, seconds later I found myself staring at an article about the place, dated May 2, 1950—more than seventy years ago.

On April 23, Mayor Anderson ordered the United Coalition's Home for Wounded Veterans to close its doors. The nursing facility for wounded veterans of World War II fell into a deep scandal earlier this year when it was revealed that a severe nursing shortage had compromised the care of numerous veterans under the government's watch.

In an ongoing investigation that spanned five months, health officials and journalists found over 300 incidents—200 incidents of outright abuse, and at least 100 health violations. All told, during a five-year span, nearly 300 deaths were estimated to be directly related to the ongoing malfeasance. Although the investigation is still active, the facility has been ordered to shut its doors and all patients have been removed from the wards and the residence halls.

The United Coalition's Home for Wounded Veterans opened in 1942 with the intent to care for wounded and traumatized veterans from the war. While the investigation only spans the time from 1945 to 1950, the Department of Health intends to do a more thorough investigation, beginning with when the facility first opened.

Discrepancies were first noted in October 1949, which led to the current investigation. Conditions were deemed intolerable, and an examination of current patients shows indications of physical and mental abuse.

One veteran, Jonathan K Smith, was first admitted to the facility in order to rehabilitate his leg. He was wounded during a skirmish in Germany. Smith, 25 at the time, was covered in bedsores and bruises. He died of septicemia on December 22, 1949. Gemma Bartlett—a nurse new to the staff— reported his death as being suspicious, which led to the current investigation. She was fired by the United Coalition's Home for Wounded Veterans two months later, for unspecified reasons, and is now suing for damages.

All patients have been moved to other nursing facilities, and the director of admissions and the director of nursing have both been arrested on charges of abuse and endangerment. Their trials are set for September 1950.

I stared at the article, then glanced at the three buildings. The facility had at one time owned the garden, which had apparently been a courtyard. From what I read, it was no wonder there were scores of the dead still here, given the psychological abuse. I flipped through my search results looking for more information. It didn't take long before I came to an encapsulation of the final result.

The United Coalition's Home for Wounded Veterans was permanently closed today as the final results of an investigation into abuse and murder was made public. Investigators named 19 members of the staff, including the director of admissions and the director of nursing, as being directly responsible for over 325 deaths during a seven-year period.

Charges are being brought against all members, excluding two nurses who turned informant. Charges range from abuse to neglect to negligent manslaughter. The court dates are being set even as this article goes to print. It was suggested that the buildings be razed, however Judge Wilkins ruled against the measure, stating there may still be evidence that will be needed during the trials. So the buildings will stand as long as needed.

I flipped through several other links, finding a brief mention from 1967, stating that the facility had been sold to a private developer who planned to build a shopping center on the land, but apparently that never happened.

Hunting some more, I discovered that the complex, including the garden, had been sold three more times, each to new developers. And each time, the plans fell through for actual development. The buildings were currently owned by the Rains Field Design Firm, although it wasn't clear what the company did. The last sale had taken place in 2008. Frowning, I dropped my phone back in my bag and slung it over my shoulder.

There had to be a reason that none of the developers ever managed to carry out their plans. My guess was that it was related to the supernatural activity. Not only was this smack in the middle of the Worchester District, but the buildings reeked with negative energy.

I stood up and walked toward the door of what had been the hospital proper, surprised to see that it wasn't boarded over.

I gazed up at the building. Four stories high, it was

made of old brick. The windows had bars on them and I wondered if it was to keep the patients in, or something out. The double doors were weathered, the gray paint peeling off. There were windows in the top half, and I was surprised to see they were unbroken. I glanced at the rest of the windows along the wall and saw that those, too, were unbroken.

I tried the knob, a worn nickel handle, but it was locked.

Damn.

If Trinity were here, he could have opened it up without a problem. But I seldom saw him during the day, and he usually didn't respond to my phone calls until after four P.M. I wasn't sure what he did or where he went, but it had been a noticeable pattern.

I tried to jiggle the knob, testing how sturdy the lock was, but it didn't budge.

Licking my lips, I stared at the lock. I had picked a few in my day, and even though I didn't pride myself on my skill, I wasn't too bad with a set of picks. For a moment, I considered calling Ember and asking her to come help me, but I wasn't sure what I was facing and I didn't want to take up her time. Herne wouldn't appreciate me pulling her off one of their cases. On the off chance that he had changed his habits, I gave Trinity a phone call, but he didn't pick up.

Finally, I decided I'd have to do it myself. I sorted through my bag and found my set of lock picks, which I always carried with me.

For non-experts, picking a lock took longer than most people thought it should, especially one as sturdy as this one appeared to be.

I glanced back at the bench, trying to gauge how heavy it was. Finally, I went over to it and dragged it over to the door so I could sit down while I was working. Luckily I was stronger than most humans, and stronger than a good number of the Fae, so I was able to drag the long stone seat over to the front of the door. A glance around showed no one watching me—no one living, at least—and so, unless I made a buttload of noise, no one should notice what I was doing.

As I went to work picking the lock, I became aware that the hairs on my neck were standing on end. Whenever that happened, I knew there were spirits nearby. And while I was well aware that the buildings were haunted, this meant that the ghosts were also patrolling the grounds. I set down my lock picks and turned around, closing my eyes as I tried to get a read on them.

A breeze swept past and I knew that it wasn't natural. I could feel something attached to it—something that hadn't been human. I probed deeper. A sweeping sense of malevolence slammed into me and I reeled back. Gasping, I steadied myself as I caught my breath.

Whatever it was, it wasn't human, which meant the situation was far more difficult than if I were dealing with a regular spirit. I wasn't sure just what it was, though, and that was another sticking point.

However, there were several things I could do.

I could try and talk to it, but given it had body-slammed me with its anger made me less inclined to try that tack. I could leave, but I didn't want to give into my fear. Or I could ignore it, hoping it would leave me alone.

I quickly walled off access to my psyche, closing my third eye to unwanted scrutiny, and focused on strengthening my shields. Ever since Pandora had managed to charm me, I had been working on my boundaries and personal wards. A few times I had wondered if it was overkill, but every time I thought of her, it spurred me on even more. I couldn't permanently erect them—that would be counterproductive to my magic—but I had learned how to slam them up at a moment's notice.

Going back to work on the lock, I fumbled around for about five minutes before hearing a click as the lock sprung open. Success!

I put the lock picks away and slung the straps of my bag over my shoulder. Slipping my hand under my skirt, I slid Venom out of her sheath, holding the dagger firmly in hand. Not that daggers usually worked against ghosts, but if there were any beasties of the mortal sort inside, at least I'd have some protection.

The door squeaked as I opened it, pushing it back slowly. Although it was bright daylight outside, inside the building the light was gloomy and dark. A good share of the windows had been boarded up, while the ones that were left clear had accumulated decades of grime on them, so the light streaming through cast only a pale glow.

I was standing in what looked like a front office, facing a built-in counter that covered two-thirds of the back wall. To either side of the counter were doors. From what I could tell, this had been a receptionist's area and waiting room.

I slowly stepped inside and shut the door behind me, shivering as I headed over to the counter. I wanted to see if anything had been left behind. It wasn't likely, given the government had been here, and the owners had probably done their best to hide any indications of wrongdoing, but it was still worth a look.

The countertop was empty, covered with dust and cobwebs. The spiders had found themselves a home, judging by the multitude of webs. I wasn't sure what they fed on until I saw a chink here and there in several of the windows. The glass wasn't fully broken, but the cracks were big enough to let insects inside, and so of course the spiders would follow. As long as they stayed in their webs, I didn't care. I didn't especially like spiders, especially after my encounter with Arachana, but they didn't frighten me.

I opened the drawers, but they were empty. Any sign of human occupation was long gone. Dusting off the chair behind the counter, I sat down, trying to suss out the energy that was swirling around me.

As I closed my eyes, I clutched Venom's hilt, just in case. I kept my boundaries up as I slowly reached out, trying to sort out the various spirits that were walking around me.

The building was thick with them, full apparitions, everywhere. They wandered the halls, wandered through the waiting room, wandered the grounds of the complex. I was trying to ferret out the one that had shrieked at me the day before, but I couldn't sense her. Very slowly, I sent out a feeler, asking if anybody there wanted to talk.

The next moment, I heard the sound of the door opening. I jerked, opening my eyes and looking at the outer door. It was still closed, but the door to my left of the counter had opened on its own. As I watched, it swung open even farther, squeaking on its hinges.

I held my breath, but nothing more happened. As I

slowly exhaled, starting to relax, the door suddenly slammed shut, shaking the walls.

I jumped and stood up, my pulse racing. I thought about asking who was there, but decided I didn't want to play that game. I had a feeling whoever was making the racket didn't want to talk; they wanted to play scare-the-ghosthunter.

Instead, I headed toward that door, walking steadily with my shoulders back. One hand on Venom, with my other hand, I reached inside my bag and pulled out a spray bottle filled with blessed water. I had gotten it from a priestess of Cerridwen in Annwn. It came from one of the sacred cauldrons that Cerridwen watched over and was good for temporarily stopping a spiritual attack.

Ghost-Be-Gone, I thought with a nervous giggle.

I approached the door, and decided the best defense was a good offense. I slid Venom through my belt so I could easily grab her, then took hold of the door handle and yanked it open, slamming the door back against the wall. As I stepped through, the door swung shut behind me. For a moment I panicked, wondering if it had locked on me, but when I tried the handle, it was still unlocked.

I turned back to the hallway.

The hall ran what looked like the length of the building—far enough so that I couldn't see the end. There were doors all along the left side, and windows along the right. The windows were barred, and here, most of them hadn't been boarded up.

The bars probably had protected them enough so that the owners decided to cut corners. And the windows looked thick, probably double pane. They were most likely strong enough to withstand a brick.

The hallway had been painted a jarring shade of mint green.

Staring at the line of doors to my left, I knew I'd never make it through all of them today, unless I did a really quick search. Sighing, I headed over to the first one and opened it. The room was filled with shelves and filing cabinets. I propped the door open using a chair that had been left in the room, and pulled open one of the filing drawers. Empty. I took a quick look through several of the others at random. They were all empty, save for a sheet of paper here or there that had escaped someone's notice. The shelves were empty as well. This had either been a supply room or a storage room for records. My bets were on the latter. I headed back out into the hall, closing the door behind me.

The next four rooms looked to be exam rooms, but again, except for the exam tables and built-in cabinets, they were fairly empty. What was left was falling apart or covered in cobwebs and grime.

I walked back into the hall, noticing that all the ghosts seemed to have vacated the surrounding area. I wasn't feeling *anybody* right now, though I knew the building was teeming with them. Frustrated, I headed down the hallway until I came to a stairwell on my left, leading up. I could either stay and explore the rest of the first floor, although I had the feeling it would be more of the same, or I could head upstairs. Pulling out my flashlight, I set foot on the first stair.

From above, around the corner of the landing, I heard a warning rumble. *Bingo.* There was something around, though I wasn't sure whether it was on the physical or spiritual plane. I wasn't sure which I preferred. I could deal easier with things on the spiritual plane, but creatures that were corporeal usually couldn't eat your life force away.

No, but they can stab you, a voice inside warned me.

Ignoring my alarm bells, I decided to head up to the second floor. My fear was probably more PTSD than anything else, and so far, while the ghosts had put up a nasty front, their bark had been worse than their bite.

Holding my flashlight in my left hand and slipping the spray bottle back into my bag, I leaned against the wall, holding onto the railing so that nothing could get past me on that side. I edged my way up the stairs, turning at the landing. As I approached the second floor, I saw a door at the top of the stairs. Hoping it wasn't locked, I eased my way up the final few stairs and tried the doorknob.

CHAPTER SEVEN

IT WAS UNLOCKED.

I yanked the door open and slipped inside, finding myself in another hallway similar to the one directly below me. Again, light streamed through the windows, while on my left there were doors running the length of the hallway. But something felt different. For one thing, there were benches along the outside wall, and I could actually see several ghosts here, some sitting on the benches and wistfully looking outside. Others seemed to be aimlessly wandering the halls. None of them seemed to notice me, and I gently reached out to try and touch their consciousness.

Nothing. I could see them, but there was no substance behind their specters. They were an imprint on time and space, a retelling of things that it happened here, like a faded filmstrip.

Most likely, the spirits had been so attached to this place—as often happened when confused people died—that they had become connected to this building and would forever wander the halls. But when I reached out, it was like I was viewing a hologram of what had happened.

I ignored them, leaving them to their peace. Some spirits faded back into the energy pool this way, not moving on to incarnate again. Usually they were either fairly new, unaware of how to manage the transition between life and death, or old—ready to let go of physical life altogether. The young ones would get trapped in their death state, but eventually their consciousnesses would fade and pass. Sometimes they were spawned new again, while other times, they just stayed within the vast universal pool of consciousness.

As I made my way down the hall, I had a sudden thought. This place was teeming with ghosts. I knew that three hundred people had died here, but it didn't make sense that they'd *all* get caught. Yet, if there were this many ghosts in this building, how many were there in the other buildings? I frowned, looking around. Most of the spirits that I could sense had been patients. That much I could tell, and given when the hospital had been built, most of them would be male. Yet I was seeing women here as well.

Could the fact that the facility was located in the Worchester District make a difference? This area *was* a magnet for ghosts, after all. But still, it didn't add up. Even in some of the most haunted areas of the world, not everybody who died ended up trapped. Unless there was something keeping them here.

Shaking my head, I slowly made my way down the hall. Some of the doors were open, some closed. From what I could tell, they had been patients' rooms. Wanting more information, I walked over to one of the benches that was unoccupied by a spirit, and sat down. The phantoms here might not notice if I sat on them, but I would feel weird about it.

I pulled out my phone again. I needed to know more about this place to understand the layout. I brought up the search again, and looked through the links until I found an article on the buildings of the United Coalition's Home for Wounded Veterans.

From what I found, two of the three buildings had been residence halls, open to returning soldiers as well as the wounded ones. They had served as transitional housing for veterans coming home from the war who didn't have a place to go.

This building had been the hospital proper. So when they had shut down the hospital, they had also shipped out those living in the transitional housing. That had probably dumped a number of veterans on the street, although by then the men would have found their way out of here. Except the majority of men had been severely traumatized—either physically or mentally—and they wouldn't have been able to heal up and get a job right away.

I was so busy looking at my phone that I lost track of what was going on around me. The next moment, a shriek to my right made me jump.

I stuffed my phone in my bag and looked down the hallway. The voice had been familiar—the one I had heard before. And there she was. She looked like an army nurse, only she was covered in blood, and there was a bullet hole on her chest, surrounded by blood. I froze as she made a beeline directly for me.

Help me, help me! Her voice echoed in my head. *It's after me! Don't let it get me!*

I reeled as she burst through my body to the other side. A wave of icy frost swept over me, chilling me to the bone. She certainly wasn't just a phantom, but a full-on spirit.

I turned but couldn't see her anymore, so I glanced over my shoulder to see if I could find out what was following her. Toward the end of the hallway, where it turned to the left, I thought I saw movement—a head peeking around the corner, perhaps.

Heading in that direction, with Venom in one hand and the bottle of blessed water in the other, I was near the bend in the hall when another shout startled me. It came from the room that I had just passed, so I headed in.

There was no light, so I had to make a decision what to keep hold of. I slid Venom into my belt and pulled out my flashlight to sweep the room. As the light hit the back wall, I saw what looked to be a word scrawled across the wall. My heart in my throat, I moved forward. Sure enough, the words "LEAVE THIS PLACE" had been written in shaky letters across the back wall. The coppery scent—blood?— was cloying and sweet in my nostrils. The blood was fresh, still dripping down the wall, and I backed up quickly, turning to race through the door as it slammed behind me.

Back in the hall, I leaned against the wall, my heart pounding. What the hell? Things like this happened with hauntings, but usually in a place where people were living, not in some abandoned hospital. I turned back around and hesitantly touched the doorknob. I tried to open the door again, but now it was locked. I backed away, glancing over at the windows that lined the wall. There, staring back at me, was the reflection of a clown—a terrifying, grotesque jester. He sneered at me, then laughed as his reflection in the window began to grow.

A series of skittering noises came from around the bend in the hall. I whirled just in time to see a swarm of rats, racing down the hallway at me. Holding out my hand, I summoned my fire.

> *Fire to flame, flame to fire,*
> *build and burn, higher and higher.*
> *Flare to life, take form in strike,*
> *attack now, fiery spike.*

A stream of fire came rushing off my hand, forming into a ball that traveled into the center of the rats and exploded. They scattered, singed by the sparks and flame. I took the opportunity to race back to the staircase as maniacal laughter filled the hallway.

I didn't look over my shoulder as I clattered down the stairs as fast as I could go. The laughter expanded to fill the hallway. I burst through the door leading into the reception room. Slamming through, I let it swing closed behind me, and kept on going toward the front door.

As I opened the door, throwing it wide, I thought I could feel bony fingers clutching at my shoulder. I jerked out of its grasp, whatever *it* was, and pulled the door shut behind me. As I stumbled away, I turned to look at the building. It was lit up with an eerie green glow. The entire building seemed alive, where before it had felt dead.

Crap, I woke something up.

My hands shaking, I sat down on the bench and pulled

out my lock picks, working to lock the door again. I wasn't sure what good it would do, and my instinct was to bolt and run, but I had to make certain that none of those things could get out on a physical level.

As I worked, holding the door shut with one hand and working the locks with the other, I could feel something trying to turn the knob from inside. My stomach lurching, I refocused my attention and finally the deadbolt shifted and turned. I was about to take my hand off the knob when something on the other side grabbed it and turned, twisting, trying to open it up. Stuffing my lock picks in my bag, I let go of the knob and slowly backed away, keeping my eyes on the door as I made my way back through the gate, shutting it behind me.

On the top floor, lights were playing through the windows.

In my attempt to help, I'd done the exact opposite. I had woken something that had been long asleep and now I had to find a way to put it back on ice. I couldn't just leave it.

I hurried back through the secret garden, walking sideways as I kept one eye on the building. I still didn't trust that whatever was in there couldn't come after me, but I made it to the chain-link fence and climbed over without further incident.

As I jogged down the side street, I wondered what the hell I was going to do. I couldn't go back there alone. Whatever it was, was too big for me to handle. I could ask Trinity, but I wasn't sure just how much he could take care of things on the spiritual level. No, I needed more help than that. I'd have to tell Kipa what I had done. And I'd probably have to approach Ember and the gang.

Dreading admitting my mistake, I made my way back to my car and sat for a moment, trying to calm down before I headed back home. I clutched the steering wheel the entire way.

I STOPPED BY THE SUN & Moon Apothecary on the way home. It was nearly two. Kipa would probably be back by now, but before I talked to him, I wanted to see if Llew might have a trick or two that I could pick up.

Llew was finishing up with a customer so I wandered over to my table and sat down. I leaned back, looking around the shop. I had taken care of a possessed doll for Jordan—Llew's husband—a few months back, and now the shop was fully warded and cleansed. Llew had been adamant about checking anything that came into the shop for psychic cling-ons.

When he finished he came over and sat opposite me. "I didn't know you were coming back today, or I could have booked you a couple clients."

"I'm not here to read the cards. Llew, I have a ghost problem."

"Isn't that your department? I don't mess with spirits if I can help it." He leaned back, crossing one leg over the other and wrapping his hands around his knee. Llew was cute, in a way, and just about the most loyal friend I could have.

"Yeah, but this… Llew, I stumbled onto an abandoned property last night and made contact with a spirit who is trapped there. Today I went back to check it out and…" I paused, frowning. I hated admitting my mistakes, but the fact was, even though my intentions were good, I had basically stirred the cauldron and now it was bubbling up and over the sides.

"What did you do?" Llew gave me a sideways glance, as though he already knew the news was bad.

"I think I unleashed something that... I don't know if it's a ghost. It might be demonic. It might be something else. But whatever it is, it chased me out. It can manifest on the physical level—I felt its hands on my shoulder."

"Oh shit. That's not good. Where is this place?"

I frowned. "Have you heard of the United Coalition's Home for Wounded Veterans? It was founded during World War II, and closed after a massive scandal revealed over three hundred unnecessary deaths, and a slew of other problems."

Llew paused for a moment, frowning. "Wait a minute. I'll be right back. Watch the counter." He disappeared into the back, behind a curtained-off doorway. I kept an eye out for customers until he returned a few moments later, holding a book. He was flipping through the pages, looking for something.

"Here it is—I thought so." He sat down and slid the book so that I could see it, too. "This is a book of local hauntings, written by an author who lives close to me. She's investigated all over the state and I can guarantee you, she's the real deal. She's a medium."

I jerked my head up. "Medium? She works with the dead?"

Llew met my gaze. He knew what I was worried about, with the rise of the dead. "I've warned her to be on her guard and I've outfitted her house with a massive number of wards and charms. I also talked her into buying a security system for the house. I check in with her at least once every other day. If Pandora or her goons are on the lookout for more victims, I won't let Lynn be one of them."

Relaxing, I leaned back. "I'll forever be watching over my shoulder, I think. At least until I grow into my full power. I talked to my mother the other night—she called. She's coming for a visit. I told her what happened and she was pissed out of her mind that I didn't let her know earlier. But she said once I reach my full power, even Pandora won't be able to stand against me. That's going to take quite a long time, though, given that I'm barely of age in my world."

Llew blinked. He had met my mother. He knew what she was like. "Give her my best," he muttered. "I hope you don't mind, but I'd rather skip any parties you throw for her. She kind of freaks me out."

I laughed. My mother was Queen of the Bean Sidhe, head servant to the Morrígan, and she freaked out a lot of people. "I'm not offended. She scares me, too, but then, I'm her daughter. She *should* be able to scare me. Anyway, what did Lynn have to say about the building?"

I leaned forward again, eyes glued to the page. There were pictures of the United Coalition's Home for Wounded Veterans in its heyday, when it was running at full capacity. Even then, there was something about the pictures that bothered me. Something that felt off.

"Lynn says here that she went in with a full investigative team. By the way, she's not one of those investigators who tries to get a rise out of the ghosts. She respects the dead, and the forces she's working with. But she does a thorough investigation both before going in and then while she's there. Anyway, she says that the building is one of the most haunted in Seattle, and that she counted at least fifty separate apparitions and handfuls of spirits there. Let's see…here it is." He adjusted the book so we could both read.

The nightmarish quality of the atmosphere struck me more than anything else—even more than the spirits I caught on camera, and the ones who were trying to communicate through me. I felt like there was something bigger hiding beneath the surface, a dark force looming behind all the spirits, keeping them trapped. I tried to tune in, but whatever it was wouldn't show itself to me. I didn't want to hold a séance because it felt like the entity was old and treacherous. Once brought to the surface, it might break through and I wouldn't be able to undo the damage. But I highly caution people: do not attempt to visit this facility. Leave it alone, and let the dead rest, even though I highly doubt they're at any semblance of peace.

Llew looked over at me. "She felt it, too. Whatever Clown Face is, she picked up on it, but she didn't try to contact it."

"Somehow, I brought its attention to myself. I wonder —maybe it's because I'm one of the Ante-Fae? I have an innate power that is noticeable by anybody who works with energy. If this creature either feeds on magical energy or is attracted by it, maybe my mere presence caught its attention?" I frowned, trying to think over the creatures that I knew fit that description. "I highly doubt that Stephen King's Pennywise has taken up residence in the building."

"Huh?" Llew asked, looking up from the book.

"You know, the clown face? I doubt it's really a clown of any sort." I paused, then sighed. "All right, I'll head home and tell Kipa. And meanwhile, can you call your friend Lynn and ask her—off the record—if there were any experiences that *didn't* make it into her book? I'm pretty sure there are a number of humans out there who, if they fully opened up about everything they had seen or experienced, would be locked away in the loony bin. And if she's a medium, chances are she may have picked up on things she didn't want to talk about."

"I'll do that in a few minutes—I'm overdue for a talk with her, anyway. I'll call you later tonight." He waved as I grabbed my bag and headed toward the door.

"Hey, if you think of anything I might need for exorcising this creature, let me know? Jot it down, pack it up, and charge my tab?"

"Will do. Bye, Raven!" He waved as the door swung shut behind me.

ALL THE WAY HOME, I tried to shake off the fear I was being followed. But whatever it was that I'd run across, it was no Pandora, and I wasn't going to be fooled again. As I pulled into my driveway, I saw Kipa's truck, so I leaped out of the car and headed for the door. The weather had shifted and it was muggy and hot, so sticky that my clothes were plastered to me. Grimacing, I unlocked the door and strode into the living room.

"Hey," Kipa said, glancing up from where he and Raj were wrestling on the floor. Kipa was letting Raj win, that much I could tell, and both of them were laughing. When he laughed, Raj got this big goofy grin on his face and he had a nasal laugh, a lot like a male Fran Drescher. It was lovable and sweet and did my heart good to hear him giggling.

They rolled to their feet, and Kipa leaped over the back of the sofa to give me a kiss. His hair was askew and falling out of his ponytail, and his shirt was sweaty, but at that moment, I threw my arms around him.

"I love you, you know that? I love that you take time with Raj, and that you...well...I love you. I'm so glad I can say it now without being afraid it's going to burst out without me realizing it." I kissed him, the funk of his sweat both enticing me and making me want to shove him into the shower. Say what they want, men didn't perspire—they *sweated*, and when they sweated, it was *fun-ky*.

"I love you too, sweet cheeks. How did things go?"

I dropped my bag on the console table back of the sofa, then hustled around to give Raj a hug. He smelled too. It had been too long since I had ordered him into the shower.

He grinned. "Raj loves Kipa. Raj loves to wrestle. Raj no wrestle with Raven or Raj would hurt Raven." He leaned back on his haunches, his eyes wide.

"Oh Raj, I know. Raven doesn't have the strength to wrestle with you. Hey, how about Raj take a bath? Get all flower fresh? Raven will turn on the water for Raj."

Usually I made him bathe outside. The cold water never bothered him, but now and then he would beg to use my violet-scented bath wash. I usually said no—he could happily use an entire bottle in one go, and I'd be cleaning up bubbles for hours. But I wanted to talk to Kipa without Raj listening in.

"Raj can smell like violets? Raj loves violets—they're so pretty and delicate." He wiggled with an excited little butt-dance.

"Yes, Raj can smell like violets." I glanced at Kipa. "Why don't you take a really quick shower in my bathroom so we can talk afterward. I'll get Raj into the bath."

I motioned for Raj to follow me and he bounced along happily by my side. Gathering the bath gel and a massive bath sheet, I led Raj into the hall bathroom and filled the tub with bubble bath. Then I tossed in Raj's toys—a plastic baby doll named Sally, a rubber duck, and a rough-and-tough plastic tank. It was an odd mix, but he somehow managed to work them all into a play session. He had recently latched onto Sally, which I had found in the thrift store. I had planned to use her for a magical project, but Raj had fallen in love with the auburn locks and princess-pretty face, so I gave him the doll and now he carried her around with him everywhere.

Raj took my hand with his as I balanced him so he could step up and over into the tub. He leaned back in the warm water, grunting with delight as the bubbles popped and frothed around him. I handed him his toys, and he hugged Sally to his chest as he leaned forward.

"Raj be good," I told him. "Raven will come back in a while to help Raj out of the bathtub."

"Raven shouldn't come back too soon, because Raj wants to destress." He closed his eyes and sighed happily.

Where he had heard that term, I wasn't sure, but Raj picked up the weirdest crap at times. Once in a while, you'd think he was Confucius. Other times, he sounded like a deranged mix-tape of rap, slang, and gibberish. I patted him on the head, heading for the door.

I turned, glancing over my shoulder. "Don't splash too much water on the floor, and don't drink the bathwater."

I had no fears he'd drown. Raj couldn't swim, but he was strong enough to pull himself out of the bathtub, so I didn't have to worry about him slipping under, and he never fell asleep in the bath. But I knew that when I returned, the bathroom would be a complete mess. All that mattered, though, was that Raj was happy, and that I had some time to talk with Kipa without Raj hearing. Because a worried gargoyle was a handful to deal with.

CHAPTER EIGHT

Kipa was out in five minutes, wearing my bathrobe. It came up to just above his knees, and the black silk looked good on him. His hair was wet, but he had brushed it back into a neat ponytail, and he gave me a quick kiss before taking a seat at the table.

"Let me get my laptop," I said. "We have some research to do. Can you pour us some wine and fix a plate of cheese and crackers to go with it?"

"Sure thing." He eyed me carefully. "Something happened, didn't it?"

"Yeah, but nothing to do with my flashbacks. I almost wish it was that. I screwed up, Kipa. I'll tell you in a moment, but I think I'm going to really need some help on this one."

Kipa smiled and for a moment I thought he was going to say, "I told you so," but he merely headed into the kitchen while I dashed down the hall to my office. I grabbed my laptop and my e-reader. If Lynn's book was in e-format, I wanted it and I wanted it *now*.

I peeked in on Raj before heading back to the table. He was splashing away, talking to his toys, and didn't even seem to notice me.

"Zinfandel all right? There was an open bottle in the fridge and I thought we could finish it off before opening a new one." Kipa had brought out the cheese, crackers, a bowl of grapes, and a package of bite-size salami rounds. He spread them on the table as I plugged in my laptop. Then he returned to the kitchen and brought back the wine and two goblets.

"Zinfandel's fine," I said, powering up the computer. I logged in and brought up a browser before helping myself to the food. Popping a grape in my mouth, I spread the port-flavored cheese spread on a handful of crackers, added salami, and then settled in for an afternoon's research.

"So, what happened?" Kipa asked as he emptied the bottle into our goblets.

I took a sip, then sighed and sat back, staring at him. "I woke something up."

His eyes narrowed. "What do you mean, you woke something up?"

"I mean, *I woke something up.*" I told him about Trinity showing me the secret garden, and then about what had happened when I broke into the place, and the book that Llew had told me about. "So yeah, there's something that's come out of hiding over there. Before you ask any questions, I want to see if I can get Lynn's book in e-format." I brought up E-Z Books, a digital bookstore, and typed in the title, which I remembered as *Haunting Seattle.* Sure enough, it popped right up and I clicked on it, then opened my e-reader and synched it to download the book.

When it finished, I searched through till I found the chapter on the United Coalition's Home for Wounded Veterans. I handed the reader to Kipa. "So, here's a picture of the place."

He glanced at the picture, then skimmed the entry. "Something old and treacherous, huh? I take it that's what you woke up?"

"Yeah, I think so. And whatever it is, it's mad as a hornet." I frowned, then began to search online for mentions of any atrocities that had happened in the area where the buildings were standing. "I'm not so great with researching," I said after a moment. "Do you think I should call Herne and ask if Yutani can give it a go? Or Talia?"

"I think so, if you want accurate information. I'm heading over there this evening—the agency is having an evening meeting on Typhon. Let me ask if you can join us." He pulled out his phone before I could respond. A moment later he stuck it back in his pocket. "You're welcome to come, Herne said. While you're there, he can talk to you about Ferosyn. I sent him a text when you agreed to talk to him."

He had acted fast. I must need more help than I thought I did. But I had asked for assistance, and I wasn't going to be angry when someone obliged.

"What time do we have to be there?"

Kipa glanced at his watch. "An hour. Why don't we head out now and we can stop for coffee on the way. Rush-hour traffic starts early."

"Let me get Raj out of the bathtub," I said. "I'll have to mop the floor, too."

While I attended to Raj, Kipa got everything together that we would need. When I came out of the bathroom, followed by a squeaky-clean gargoyle, all I had to do was make sure the wards and the security system were working and armed, and follow Kipa out the door.

THE WILD HUNT Agency was on First Avenue, in the Old Town section—which had once been known as the Pioneer Square area. The place was like a gracious lady once rich, who was now old and poor. An echo of gentility and beauty was still there over the grimy underbelly, like a pretty painting covering up a dark, ugly blotch.

A series of fetish brothels and small takeout places lined the street opposite the brick building in which the agency was housed, and the wide staircase had been painted by graffiti artists. The superintendent had given up trying to fight it, Ember had told me, and finally paid the kids to do one hell of a gorgeous depiction of the staircase ascending through the clouds.

There was a side ramp offering handicapped access—that was new—and at the top of the stairs, old double wooden doors led into the first floor. The elevator was near the urgent care clinic that took over most of the main floor, but from what I remembered, it was in and out of order. Not feeling like getting stuck in a small car, we decided to take the stairs to the fourth floor, where we rang the buzzer that led into the waiting room.

Angel was sitting at the desk, reading. She glanced up and waved. "Raven! Hey, I didn't know you were coming with Kipa."

"Yeah, I need some advice, so Kipa asked Herne if I could tag along." I accepted the muffin she pressed into my hand.

Angel was an extraordinary cook and baker, and she liked it when people ate. I had no more than taken one bite when Herne called us all into the break room. I followed Angel back, waving at Ember, who was over by the coffee pot as usual. I drank a lot of caffeine, but Ember put me to shame. She pointed to the coffee but I shook my head. I had had quite enough adrenaline for the day. Herne was talking in low tones to Yutani and Talia, but when he saw me he walked over and held out his hand.

"Welcome, Raven. Kipa said you had something happen today that you needed some advice on?" He got down to the point, that was for sure.

I nodded. "Yeah, actually I think it's a serious situation and I'm afraid I might not be the only one dealing with the fallout, so I thought I'd come and ask for your advice."

"We're starting up in a moment. You can go first, so you don't have to sit through all of our old business. I'm going to need Kipa, though, so unless you drove your own car you can either stick around for the rest of our meeting, or wait for him in the reception area."

"How long is your meeting going to run?" It occurred to me that, while waiting, I could do some shopping at the deli across the street.

"Probably about forty-five minutes. We have a couple issues we have to tackle." He paused, then motioned me off to the corner of the room so the others couldn't hear.

"By the way, Kipa told me you've asked to speak to Ferosyn. I passed along the information and he will be getting in touch with you in the next day or so. I think you made a wise decision. He helped Rafé a great deal."

I glanced around, spying Rafé over by Angel. He worked for the Wild Hunt now as a clerk. And even though I hadn't had a chance to talk to him for a while, he looked a lot calmer than he had the last time I had seen him. Rafé had been Ulstair's brother, and we kept in close contact still. He glanced up, as though sensing my gaze on him, and gave me a little wave. I did the same.

I turned back to Herne. "Thank you. I thought I could get over it myself, but apparently even the Ante-Fae have our limits."

"If you'll pardon me saying so, and take it for what it's worth, but it's also your age. Raven, you may be Ante-Fae, but you're still young. There's still so much that you haven't had time to experience, and there's a lot of ugliness in this world along with the beauty. Sometimes even the strongest of us need someone to talk to."

With that, he placed his hand on my shoulder and guided me to the table.

Herne and Kipa were two of a kind, and yet they were so different. I knew they were about the same age, but Herne seemed almost older, more mature. Kipa was more passionate and closer to the wild. Kipa pulled out my chair for me and I slid into it.

"What did Herne say?" he asked.

"He told me that Ferosyn will contact me as soon as possible." I squeezed his hand, bringing it to my lips to kiss it.

"First order of business," Herne said. "Kipa has asked if

Raven could address the Wild Hunt. Something's happened and she needs our advice. I told him to bring her along tonight."

Those who hadn't had a chance to greet me—Yutani, Viktor, Talia, and Charlie—murmured their hellos. I waved at them in return.

"Why don't you go ahead and tell us what's going on? And then we'll see what we can do." Herne motioned for me to take the floor.

I bit my lip, dreading telling them what I had done, but there was no help for it. I knew I needed guidance on this, and it wouldn't do to hide it.

"I'm afraid that I may have woken something up. While it's certainly no Typhon, I still think it could do a lot of damage." I quickly proceeded to tell them everything that had happened.

"Obviously, I don't think it's a clown, but whatever it is, it's dangerous." I brought out my e-reader, bringing up Lynn's book. "Here's a mention of the place in *Haunting Seattle*. The author herself noted she felt something there beneath the surface. Unlike my smartass self, she had the wisdom not to bother it." I handed the e-reader to Ember, who was sitting to my left. She scanned it, then handed it over to Yutani, who read the passages aloud.

Herne just stared at me, shaking his head. "What was your game plan?"

I shrugged. "I knew there was some spirit trapped there, and I thought maybe she was just bound because of the place or some sort of hex or something like that. I had no idea I was waltzing into spiritpalooza."

"What did you do to wake it up?" Talia asked.

"I have no idea. I didn't try any rituals. I did cast one

spell, but that was after it was already awake and sent a swarm of rats at me. I'm wondering if just my presence woke it up? I have a strong aura, and I am a bone witch. I carry the mark of Arawn in my aura. Maybe that was enough?"

Angel shifted in her seat. "Well, I hate to tell you this, but you're carrying some of the creature's energy with you. It's not exactly like it followed you, but I can sense that it's draining off some of your energy even now."

Angel was an empath, and I knew she was training in the magical arts with Ember's mentor. I had learned to trust what she said.

"Oh, that's just hunky-dory. What do I do about that?"

"Don't you cleanse your chakras regularly?" She stared at me like I had just told her I didn't bathe.

I shrugged. "I keep my wards up, but no, I don't think I've ever given my chakras a bath." I tried to keep it light-hearted, but she rolled her eyes and jumped up from the table.

"Hold on a moment." She vanished out the break room door.

I turned to Yutani, who was already poking through his computer. "I was wondering if you could find out any information on that land. Whatever this is, it feels older than those buildings and older than the veterans who are trapped there."

"I think you're right," he said. "The Worchester District has always been the most haunted area in Washington state, and quite frankly, from what I'm seeing here, the entire area was considered off-limits to the Native Americans who lived here before the settlers came in."

I frowned, about to say something when Ember spoke up.

"Really? Why?"

"It appears that there has always been some sort of vortex in that area. It doesn't extend very far out—only as big as the district itself, but that's still good-enough size to attract some very negative energies. There were legends here that anyone who lived in that area too long would go mad. In fact, one of the shifter tribes who lived on the land since before Seattle was founded used to lock up their lawbreakers there."

"Which shifter tribe?" Herne asked.

"The Alpha Marta Wolf Clan. There aren't many of them left; they appear to either have assimilated into other wolf shifter packs, or died out. There are a few descendants who belong to the North Forest Wolf Shifter pack, located in the Greenwood area." Yutani glanced over the entry he was reading. "The Alpha Marta pack built an enclosure in the Worchester District, right around the area where the veterans home is located. They locked up the worst of their offenders there, basically leaving them to each other. They would occasionally throw food in for them, but the prisoners were never set free, and most of them died of unnatural causes."

Kipa grimaced. "What do you mean, 'unnatural causes'?"

"Well, legends say that a couple of the prisoners ripped out their own eyeballs and died of the resulting infection. The prisoners turned on each other a lot, but there's some mention of the Lykren, a shape-changing creature of immense proportions that ate souls and flesh, and fed on fear."

Yutani glanced up, his eyes dark. "Ten to one, the legends were real and the Lykren just went into stasis. It says here it would seem to vanish for years and then it would be active for a period of time before going back into hibernation. Let's see, if it was active when the hospital was there, that was about seventy years ago. Let me check what happened in that area around 1870 to 1880."

I bit my lip, thinking about what he had said. "You mean there's a chance that I didn't actually wake it up? That it's just running on a cycle and I stumbled in at the perfect time?"

"I think that's exactly what happened." Yutani glanced up at me, pointing to his computer. "In 1869, that area was established as a large church and religious school. No sooner had it opened than it burned down in a great fire that was prescient of the fire that would destroy the good share of Seattle twenty years later. But when the church went down, elders of the Alpha Marta pack warned the settlers not to reestablish it. They had been shunted off the land, obviously, but the church and the religious school were directly over where they had kept their prison, so to speak."

"Did anyone die in the fire?" I asked.

Yutani nodded. "Three priests, four nuns, and twenty-eight children who had moved into the religious boarding school. I don't know if the church believed what the shifter clan told them or not. But they found another place to rebuild and that area was left empty for quite some time."

Ember leaned forward. "Do you think that the Worchester District is haunted because of this Lykren?"

Yutani shook his head. "No. I think the Lykren was attracted by the energy there. Since the area is one big natural vortex, it most likely attracts all sorts of psychic phenomena. It's chaotic, to say the best. There's nothing anybody can do to shut it down, I think. That sort of natural convergence of ley lines is best left untouched. What would be best is if nothing was built in the area and it was just left alone."

"From what I understand, several developers bought the complex, but none of them have ever developed the area. They just sell it off again. Do you think that the energy isn't conducive to building new malls or shops? That it's sort of forcing the developers to give up?"

"I think perhaps the Lykren is the one who's doing that. This creature—entity—from what I can find, tries to present itself as your worst nightmare. Are you afraid of clowns?" Yutani gave me an odd look, the corners of his lips turning up just little.

I blushed. "Who isn't?"

"Then that's why you saw a giant clown face in the window. Hell, given what happened, I'm surprised you didn't see Pandora's face."

I froze, clutching the edge of the table with my hands as my breath caught in my chest.

"Think before you speak," Herne warned, giving Yutani an irritated look.

Startled, Yutani glanced up, catching my gaze. A stricken look spread over his face and he scrambled to apologize. "I'm so sorry. I didn't even think—"

"Obviously," Ember said. She reached out and took my left hand, holding it tightly between her palms. Kipa put his hand on my shoulder, rubbing gently.

I fought down a wave of panic. For some reason, the mention of her name like that—from out of the blue—had caught me off guard. I struggled for a moment more, finally letting out a slow stream of breath as I tried to relax.

"I guess I need to talk to Ferosyn more than I thought I did," I murmured.

"He'll call you by tomorrow at the latest, I promise you that." Herne again glanced at Yutani and shook his head. "Dude, you have to work on your social skills. You're brilliant, but you lack even the basic social graces."

"He's also cute," Talia said.

"Cute, but stupid." Yutani rubbed his forehead, brushing his hair back from his face. As he swept it back into a ponytail and wrapped it with a hair tie from his pocket, he let out a slow breath and looked at me again. "I really do apologize. I didn't mean anything by it, I hope you realize that."

"Well," I said, "if the Lykren appears as your worst nightmare, and it showed up as a clown for me, maybe Pandora isn't quite at the bottom of the barrel for me. The truth is, when I was little there was an Ante-Fae who lived in the same territory as my father. He was called the Harlequin. And he scared the shit out of me. He was one of those Ante-Fae who makes us *all* look bad. He was a child eater, and it didn't matter whether it was a shifter kid or human, or even another of the Ante-Fae, he would lure them into the wooded areas around Hanging Hills and then eat them alive. My father used to scare me with those stories so much that I never misbehaved in terms of running away or going off into the woods alone."

"The Harlequin? I've heard of him. He's still out there,

isn't he?" Herne shook his head. "If you lived near him when you were a child, no wonder that's the image that the Lykren took for you. Pandora may be a psychopath, but somehow I don't think she's quite as dangerous as the Harlequin is."

I managed to laugh, and the tension in the room broke. "As much as I loathe Pandora, I think I'd rather go up against her again than the Harlequin." I paused, then continued. "Okay, what do I do about the Lykren? I feel better now that I know that I didn't wake it up, but something has to be done about it. And I think it's holding all those souls hostage."

"No, the vortex is trapping them. At least some of them. But I agree with you, the Lykren should be addressed. And you can't do it alone. He's old and crafty, and like a sleeping lion, something that you should just leave alone if you can." Yutani bit his lip. "Meanwhile, one of the most important things to do is find where he makes his lair there. Because even though he works on the astral a lot, the Lykren is a physical entity."

I perked up. "You mean we can actually kill him?"

Kipa snorted. "You never really think in terms of *trapping* something, do you?"

I shrugged. We had had this conversation before and he never won. "If you have a tumor, you take it out. You don't leave it around. What the hell would you expect to do with this thing? If you transported it somewhere where there aren't any people, it's just going to find its way back to where there are people. It feeds on pain and fear, as well as apparently energy. The Lykren isn't going to find a buffet in a grizzly bear."

Laughing, Kipa shrugged. "Point taken. Okay, how do

we destroy this? And who's up for helping us, because I'm not about to let Raven do this herself?"

"Right now, Yutani and Talia and I are tied up on another case. I can let you have Ember and Viktor for a few days. Will that work?" Herne asked.

I nodded eagerly. "Thank you. All the help I can get is welcome. Trinity might be interested in helping as well. Hey, do you think Meadow and Trefoil O'Ceallaigh would have information on this creature? They belong to LOCK."

"It can't hurt to ask," Kipa said. "If they're still up when we get home we can talk to them. If not, we can go over there tomorrow."

"Did you say that you were going to ask Trinity to help?" Herne gave me a long look.

I nodded. "We've been hanging out a lot since what happened up on the mountain. I get along with him pretty well." I noticed a look flash between Herne and Kipa, then Herne turned back to me.

"Just be cautious around him. He's helped me several times in the past, and it's not that he's a dangerous person, but..." He trailed off, then shrugged. "Just be cautious, that's all I ask."

I frowned. "First Vixen warns me about him, now you. What is the deal with Trinity? Why does everybody seem to dislike him and why won't anybody tell me the reason?"

Herne shook his head. "Never mind. It's not my place to tell you who to hang out with and who to avoid. Just be careful how much you get involved with him."

I was really frustrated with people giving me warnings and then not telling me why. But I could tell Herne wasn't going to say another word about it. I would just have to pump Vixen or Trinity himself for the information I wanted. I shrugged, then stood up.

"All right, why don't you guys figure out when you can meet with me tomorrow, and then have the rest of your meeting. I'm going to go shopping across the street for some groceries. You have some delis down here that we don't have near my house."

Kipa pulled me to him, standing to give me a kiss before I left. I waved at the others and then headed out the door. Angel accompanied me to unlock the stairwell door for me. They kept both the elevator and the stairwell door locked during the time they were in their meetings. I turned to her before I left.

"So counseling really helped Rafé?"

She nodded. "If he hadn't gone, I would have left him by now. He was becoming too volatile and unpredictable." She paused for a moment, then continued. "If what happened to you is creating a wedge between you and Kipa, please ask for help. You two make a good pair, and I'd hate to see you break up because of what someone else did. You can't ever erase what happened, Raven, but you can put it behind you. You just need help in learning how to do that."

Impulsively, I gave her a quick hug and kissed her on the cheek. "Thank you. Really, I mean it." And then I turned, and headed down the stairs to go shopping.

CHAPTER NINE

I HAD JUST FINISHED SHOPPING AT KLEIN'S DELI AND carried my bags out, preparing to cross the street back over to the Wild Hunt, when a sudden chill raced through me and I sensed a spirit run by. I quickly turned, catching sight of the ghost as it dashed into one of the fetish brothels. What the hell? What was a spirit doing downtown in a sex shop?

I was about to ignore it when I heard a sudden shriek from inside the shop. I didn't want to deal with anything else tonight, but decided I should go take a look. The shop was called Kink in Boots, and the menu posted on the window promised a wide selection of sexy times combined with leather, high heels, whips, chains, and harnesses. Grinning, I pushed through the door, glancing around.

The reception area—if you could call it that—was tastefully decorated, with black leather furniture and light oak side tables. On the walls were framed prints, each a picture of one of the available sex workers at the shop. A large framed plaque in back of the counter spelled out the rules, leaving no question as to the fact that they took their safety seriously. The counter ended at a wall, with a locked door to the side leading into the nether regions of the shop.

A man sat on one of the leather sofas, reading a book as he waited, and a woman behind the counter was decked out in black leather bondage gear. A Taser sat on the counter beside her, along with a computer, a phone, and a bowl of after-dinner mints. The walls were painted a soft green, and all in all, except for the pictures and the receptionist's uniform, it could have been a waiting room for any number of different shops.

The receptionist was frowning, staring over at the corner near the front window. I glanced at the corner and saw the ghost, leaning against the wall with a smirk on his face. Oh great, a smartass spirit. I could recognize them just about anywhere by their attitudes. I turned to the receptionist.

"I take it you have a ghost problem?" I was too tired to make small talk.

She nodded. "Yeah. He won't leave the shop alone, and he's been bothering us for the past couple years. I've asked the owner if I could bring in an exorcist, but he doesn't want freak out the customers." She glanced over at the man sitting on the sofa. He wasn't paying any attention to us, keeping his eyes on his e-reader. I got the feeling he was embarrassed to be seen here and wasn't about to voluntarily participate in any conversations.

"Do you want me to see if I can take care of him? It's

kind of what I do." I held out my hand to her and she shook it. "I'm Raven BoneTalker, by the way."

"I'm Nancy. I'm afraid I'm not authorized to pay you anything." She paused, then added, "But hey, I'll give you what I've got my pocket if you'll help. Well, my purse, since I am obviously not wearing any pockets. I just want that spirit out of here. He drives me nuts."

I set my groceries down on the counter. "Don't worry about the money. Let me see what I can do."

I turned back to the spirit, heading in his direction. He straightened up, suddenly aware that I was staring straight at him. I could see the surprise on his face. Oh yeah, I had dealt with his kind before. Some spirits weren't malicious but had a twisted sense of humor, and they enjoyed aggravating the living. They wouldn't deliberately hurt anybody, but they did like to play jokes and tricks, and essentially scare people. I wasn't sure what went into making up their psyches when they were still alive, but I had a feeling a number of them were your typical high school bully types and they never grew out of it.

I let out my breath slowly, then closed my eyes and conjured up my web spell. It wasn't an actual spider's web, but it acted like in an etheric net, in which I would be able to catch spirits who weren't too powerful. I held out my hands, focusing on the energy as I wove the web between them.

> *Weave the web, weave the spell,*
> *as I now do compel*
> *spirit, spirit, enter the web*
> *as I call and trap the dead.*

You cannot run, you cannot hide.
For you are dead and I'm alive.
For you are weak and I am strong
and my web is wide and long.

I trap thee now and you will come
you cannot flee, you cannot run
into my web I now command
as I finish the last strand.

I finished weaving the etheric web and cast the spell as I did so, watching as the ghost suddenly jerked toward me. He was fighting the magic, but he wasn't very strong, and I could feel the power of Arawn flow through me. The Lord of the Dead was more powerful than just about any other god, and none of the living could ever withstand him. None of the dead could fight against him.

The spirit let out a strangled obscenity, something like *fuck you*, but he slid into the web as I bound it around him, weaving the strands tightly together so that they covered him entirely.

"Yeah, yeah, tell it to the judge," I muttered. I could carry him like this until I decided what to do with him, but it would help if I had some sort of container in which to lock his essence. I turned back to the receptionist.

"Hey Nancy, you wouldn't happen to have some sort of box, or even a bag, would you? A box would be best."

She was watching with wide eyes. Apparently she could see the spirit and what he was doing. She fumbled around behind the counter and brought out a small trinket box. It was cute, with a ladybug on top, and it was about four inches square. "Will this work? It's what I keep my rings in, but I can find something else if it won't."

I nodded, accepting the box. I took the lid off and then focused on pushing all the energy of my web spell, along with the trapped spirit, into the box. A small gelatinous ooze appeared against the bottom of the box, which told me that I had been successful. I replaced the lid and turned back to her.

"Do you have a rubber band? I don't want the lid to come off while I'm on the way home."

She nodded, speechless. She handed me a rubber band and I wrapped it around the box several times.

"Okay, I've got him trapped. I'll take him home and move him onto the Phantom Kingdom. From there, he can make his way across the Veil. I doubt he'll return, but if he manages to find his way back, just give me a call." I fumbled in my purse and brought out one of my business cards, handing it to her.

"Thank you, I really appreciate this. Are you sure I can't pay you something for your business?"

I shook my head. "Consider it pro bono. Although if you ever know anybody looking for tarot readings, my number's on there. The second number is the number of the shop where I do most of my readings. You can call them and Llewellyn will book you a time, or you can call me." I winked at her. "Random ghost-busting has actually been good to me in the past in terms of finding clients," I added with a grin.

She laughed. "No problem. And if you ever want any of our services, or you have a friend who's into a little latex, just call me and I'll set them up for a freebie." She handed me a card for the shop, writing her own number on the back. "Again, thank you. I've been dealing with that spirit for the past three years. He loves coming in and disrupting things."

"Well, I doubt if he'll do that again. I'll talk to you later," I said, waving at the strawberry blonde as I headed out of the shop. The man on the sofa glanced up at me, then went back to his reading, apparently unfazed.

As I crossed the street, dusk was falling and the streeps had begun packing up to go back to their flops. I sat on the stairs leading up to the building, enjoying the warm evening air. A few moments later, Ember and the rest exited the building, chattering loudly. Kipa took the groceries from me as I stood.

"I hope you weren't waiting out here too long." He gave me a kiss.

I laughed. "I found something to amuse myself." I turned to Ember and Viktor. "Can you two come over tomorrow to talk about the secret garden area?"

Ember nodded. "Actually, why don't you meet us at the office here at eleven? Will that work?"

I nodded. "Sure thing. See you then."

As we headed toward the parking garage, I was about to tell Kipa what had happened when my phone rang. I glanced at the caller ID. *Ferosyn.* It still boggled me how the gods used cell phones, and how they managed to find some way to call from Annwn. I hadn't figured out how yet, but someday I was going to sit down and make Herne explain it all to me.

Answering, I held the phone close to my ear. "Raven here."

"Herne said that you're interested in talking to one of my therapists. I think that's a good idea. Can you come over to Annwn tomorrow afternoon? Say around three P.M.?"

"To Cernunnos's Palace?"

"Yes, that would be best."

"All right. I'll see you then. Where should I go?"

"Just show up at the Healing Center. They'll be waiting for you and they'll bring you right to me. I'll leave notice that you're on the way at the front."

I said good-bye, then stuffed my phone back in my pocket. "Well, apparently I start therapy tomorrow," I told Kipa. "I have to go over to Annwn in the afternoon. So I'll need to go to a portal. I suppose I could use one in TirNa-Nog, but those tend to be pointed toward the great Fae cities. I need to call Herne and ask him if I can use one of the portals to his father's palace."

"He's right behind us. Why don't you run back and ask him now?"

I jogged back to where Herne and Ember were walking together. "Herne, Ferosyn just called. I need to be at your father's palace tomorrow. Can I use one of the Wild Hunt portals? I'd rather not have to take a round-about way." There were other portals around the area besides the ones that Herne had control over, but I trusted his to get me where I needed to go.

"Of course you can. In fact, there's one near my house. I'll make arrangements for you to use it tomorrow. What time do you need to be there?"

"Ferosyn wants me there at three, at the Healing Center. I can come over and hang out with Ember and

Viktor, discuss the case at eleven, and then go through to Annwn after that."

"I tell you what, I need to go talk to my mother tomorrow afternoon. I'll escort you to the palace. And I'm sure Ferosyn will have someone who can escort you back. Will that work?" He gave me a lazy grin that told me he didn't mind at all.

"Thank you, I appreciate it. Okay, I'll see you tomorrow morning, around eleven."

After saying good-bye again to both Ember and Herne, I headed back to where Kipa was waiting in the car. I climbed in his truck, pulling the door shut. As I fastened my seatbelt and leaned back, I wondered what therapy would be like. But then again, it couldn't be as bad as the flashbacks that I was having. And it couldn't be as bad as what Pandora had put me through. Or at least, I hoped it wouldn't.

THE NEXT MORNING, after tending to the ferrets, I carried the box with the spirit into my ritual room. As I settled down in front of the altar, I placed the box in front of Arawn's statue.

"Blessed Arawn, Lord of the Dead, guide and guard me in my journeys. Blessed Cerridwen, Keeper of the Sacred Cauldron of Rebirth, guard and guide me in my journeys. Teach me to walk in the shadows without fear, for I am the Daughter of Bones, speaker for the dead. Guide me through the Aether as I perform my duties. Strengthen me, swallow my fear, let me walk with confidence and surety. Blessed be the Guardians of the Underworld. So Mote It Be."

The litany was comforting and I lowered myself into trance. A few moments later, I could feel them standing before me. Or perhaps, my spirit was standing before them. Either way, I reached out and picked up the box, holding it up in front of the altar.

"Lord Arawn, I have here a spirit who has been bothering the living. He belongs in the Phantom Kingdom. Please take him in, guide him through the Veil, show him what he needs to do next."

I opened the box, and I could feel the psychic web that I had created unraveling as Arawn coaxed the spirit out, gently guiding him into the underworld. A moment later, the man was gone.

"Thank you, Lord Arawn and Lady Cerridwen."

I paused, realizing it had been a while since I had done anything in front of my altar for my gods. I had been reluctant, not wanting to face them after what Pandora had done to me. It dawned on me that I had been blaming them—punishing both them and myself. I took a deep breath, and thought over what I wanted to say.

"I apologize, and I ask for your forgiveness. I have been neglectful of my duties, and I have been neglectful of acknowledging your presence. I realize that I was angry at you. When I called out for help, neither of you came. But I know that's not something that you can always do. It's not something I have the right to expect. And maybe you *did* show up—maybe you were the guiding force that led Ember to where I was being held. Maybe you worked through her."

I paused for a moment, then added, "Whatever the

case, I apologize for blaming you for what happened. It wasn't your fault."

I was crying, I realized. Tears were dripping down my face. Grateful for waterproof mascara and eyeliner, I looked at the skull that sat between Cerridwen and Arawn's statues. Sometimes working for the gods who watched over death was a heavy mantle to wear. I had been steeped in spirits and ghosts and graveyards and headstones since I was little. I was born a bone witch, and part of it was directly related to my mother being Queen of the Bean Sidhe. My father, too, dealt in meting out death, even though it wasn't something over which he had control. My entire family was born from the grave.

"You have been with me since the day I was born, haven't you?"

I wasn't expecting an answer. But a moment later, the light dimmed in the room and a tall man appeared before me. He filled the room from floor to ceiling, and he appeared to be standing directly through my altar. He was massively built, and his skin was a deep, rich brown. His hair flowed down his shoulders, down to his lower back. He had a neatly trimmed beard and mustache, and he was wearing a black robe studded with silver stars and a silver headdress, a diadem with a crystal skull in the center. The stars on his robe twinkled as he moved and the scents of autumn lingered in the air around him, of harvest leaves and bonfires, of cinnamon and apple cider and caramel.

"My young priestess, I have been with you long before you were born. You do not remember your time with me in the halls of my castle, but trust me, you were with me then, and you will be with me again. For now, know that even though we cannot always step in directly, the Lady

Cerridwen and I are always with you, in your heart, and in the depths of your soul. And yes, we did indeed guide Ember to finding you."

And then, before I could say a word, he reached out and stroked my cheek, his touch as cold as the frozen north, and as desolate as a wasteland. And then he vanished.

I caught my breath. I had heard Arawn and Cerridwen before, talking to me, and they lived always in my heart, but this was the first time I had ever seen the Lord of the Dead in all of his glory. Overcome by the residue of his power, by the touch that still stung my cheek with its icy brilliance, I burst into tears. I rested my head on my arms, leaning on the altar, and cried my eyes out, freeing the pain and fear that I had locked away.

As cold as the God of Death was, he also had a warmth that I couldn't explain, and a gentleness that belied his strength. I wept as though my life depended on it, and finally, when I was able to catch my breath, I sat up and wiped away my tears. My breath felt freer than it had been in weeks, and I wanted to sleep, possibly for days. But I didn't have time for a nap, so I kissed the statues of Arawn and Cerridwen and headed out of my ritual room, stopping to wash my face and reapply my makeup before I went to eat breakfast with Kipa.

EMBER AND VIKTOR were waiting for me when I arrived at the Wild Hunt. Kipa hadn't come with me; he had another errand to run for Herne and told me he would see me at home.

Angel motioned for me to go through to Ember's office, so I followed the hallway back to the end. Viktor was sitting in a chair near Ember's desk, and I took a seat on the sofa beneath the window that overlooked the alley. Ember had opened the window, but the scent of garbage was starting to seep into the room and apologetically, she closed it as I sat down.

"I'm sorry, I forgot that garbage day isn't until tomorrow and there's quite a buildup down there in the dumpsters. Let me turn on a fan." She switched on a large fan so it would move the air around the room. "I didn't realize it was going to get so warm today."

"Yeah, it's supposed to get up to eighty-one today. I don't know about you, but I could go for some rain. It's been warm for several weeks and we need a break. Also, have you noticed how muggy it's getting? We're due for a storm."

As the fan turned my way, the blast of cool air hit me and I shook my hair out. I had chosen a short black skirt that came to mid-thigh, beneath which I was wearing patterned tights that stopped at my ankles, and a fitted purple corset top. It had acrylic bones and zipped up the front, and the material was light enough so that it wasn't too warm to wear. My birthmarks that covered my shoulders and arms and back were visible, and you could see the birthmarks on my chest as well. A pair of purple ballerina flats completed the outfit.

I slid my shoes off and crossed my legs on the sofa. "Okay, so what do we do about the Lykren?"

"First, let's go over everything that we know again." Ember brought up all of Yutani's research and we went over everything point by point. It didn't add much to our knowledge base, but it established the known facts. An hour later, she poured us coffee while I stared at the map of the Worchester District.

"There sure are a lot of ley lines running through that sector. I wonder why." I pointed to the center of the district, which was a few blocks from the abandoned veterans home. "This appears to be ground zero for the vortex."

"Yes, and it's only growing stronger. We contacted LOCK this morning before you came in, and they confirmed that psychic activity has picked up in the district over the years, growing by over fifty percent—if you count reported incidents." Ember frowned, staring at the graph. "It would be interesting to find out why, but I'm afraid that's a case for another day."

"What now?" I asked. "We need to go in armed, and prepared to deal with the myriad ways of attack that the creature has. It's like the Swiss army knife of monsters."

"I guess we go in with as many weapons as we can carry and play it by ear. You'll have to lead us."

"Do you guys mind if I ask Trinity to go with us?" I asked. "I wish I knew why Herne and Vixen were so hesitant about him. He's been nothing but good to me over the past weeks."

Ember hesitated. "I know you like him, but I'll be honest. For some reason he makes me uncomfortable. I don't know why. Herne hasn't told me anything or I would tell you. He just strikes me as chaotic, I guess."

"Just think about it, all right?" I frowned, then shrugged. "When do you want to go over there? I don't have time this afternoon, given Ferosyn wants me at his office at around three."

"Tomorrow morning? I'm not about to go out there in the dark," Ember said.

"That works for me," Viktor said. "And it will give Ember and me a chance to take a look to see if we can find the blueprints to the facilities. If we know the layout, it will help when we go in. I'm not sure we'll be able to get hold of them, but we'll try."

"Shall I meet you here at around nine?" I asked. "I know you always have a staff meeting first thing in the morning."

We agreed on meeting at nine, and I headed out, telling Herne I'd be back by about two. It was twelve-thirty, and though they asked me to stay and eat lunch with them, I wanted to take care of a couple other errands.

As I left the building, the streeps were out in full force, and it was so muggy that my clothes felt plastered to my skin. I glanced up at the sky. Even though it was clear I could feel thunder in the offing, and I hoped that it would come soon to break the heat.

I headed across the street to return the ladybug box to Nancy. She wasn't there, so I left it with a note for her at the front desk and headed out again. I thought about contacting Trinity but decided to wait. Instead, I drove over to the docks, and walked out on the boardwalk to watch the ferries leave from the pier. As the seagulls dipped and swept through the air, waiting for the chance to grab a spare crumb from one of the numerous people on the boardwalk, I let the cool breeze coming off the water slide past me, bracing me up.

There were days when I loved the city, when I loved being on the water, and this was one of them. Behind me,

Seattle hustled through the muggy day, the streeps playing music on the crowded sidewalks, the cars congesting the roadways and everywhere the persistent throngs of shoppers and bicyclists zooming by who were the lifeblood of the city itself. Yes, the city was beautiful even with a layer of darkness beneath it. And I was part of the darkness, part of the shadow side, and so part of the whole.

CHAPTER TEN

At two p.m., Herne texted me to ask me where I was. I texted back that I was outside, sitting on the stoop of the building, getting some fresh air. He answered that he'd be down in just a moment, so I gathered my things. Sure enough, less than a couple minutes later, he came clattering down the stairs, looking rough, tough, and ready to rumble.

Herne was handsome, I'd give him that. He had long wheat-colored hair and cornflower blue eyes. He had a scruff of a beard, more of a five-o'clock shadow, actually. He was wearing black jeans and a cobalt blue tank top, over which he had tossed a black leather jacket. It looked light, made for summer rather than for the cooler months. And he was wearing a pair of motorcycle boots, his jeans tucked into them.

"Do you have anything else you need to take with you?" He looked around.

I shook my head. "Just my purse. Is it okay to leave my

car in the parking garage? We won't get back too late for me to get it out, will we?"

"I think it should be fine. And if worse comes to worse, I can drive you home and then pick you up in the morning and bring you over to get your car." He jogged across the street, and I followed at a slower pace. We walked the half block to the parking garage, where he unlocked the passenger door to his Ford Expedition and held it open as I scrambled inside. As I fastened my seatbelt, he swung into the driver's seat and fitted the key in the ignition.

"How did the meeting with Ember and Viktor go?"

I shrugged. "We're heading up to the veterans home tomorrow. Listen, Herne, will you *please* tell me what you have against Trinity? I like to think that I give people a fair chance, and so far Trinity's been nothing but considerate to me. But you warned me about him, and Vixen's warned me about him. If you guys want me to avoid him, you're going to have to give me a good reason, other than you don't trust him. After all, you're the one who brought him into my life."

Herne let out a sigh. "I knew you were going to ask that. I've struggled with this all night. I'd tell you willingly, except it's Trinity's secret and I feel like I'm invading his privacy. But in the interest of friendship, I'll tell you why I have misgivings, and yet can say that I like the man." He flipped the turn signal and moved into the left lane. "We're headed to the portal near my home, by the way. It's in the park behind my house, just a few yards over the property line. I've contacted Orla, who's preparing it to transport us to Cernunnos's Palace."

I nodded, waiting for his story.

"All right, about Trinity. First, I *do* like Trinity, and he's helped me out a number of times. And he's never once asked for a reward, or payment. I think he just gets off on the adrenaline—he's a big adrenaline junkie."

"I can relate," I said.

"Right. But Trinity is…*special*, even among the Ante-Fae. And I think that's what causes your friend Vixen to dislike him so much. Trinity is *more* than Ante-Fae."

"What do you mean, more than Ante-Fae?" As far as I could tell, Trinity wasn't of mixed heritage. But maybe he had some sort of glamour to hide it.

"You've noticed that Trinity's titles include not only the Keeper of the Keys, but the Lord of Persuasion?"

Again, I nodded. "Right. He's able to get through most locks. I don't know what the persuasion part is about."

"While Trinity is Ante-Fae by nature and blood, his father was possessed by an incubus when he impregnated Trinity's mother, and some of that essence passed on to Trinity himself. So Trinity is also part incubus, on a soul level. That's where the Lord of Persuasion comes in. His father was Maximus, one of the minor lords of the incubi. He seduced Trinity's mother, and quite frankly, I'd call it rape. He used his charm on her. Otherwise she would have said no."

I frowned, staring out the window. "But that's not Trinity's fault."

"No, but he carries the darkness of his father within him."

I didn't say anything for a moment as I processed what Herne had told me. Finally, I asked, "Who is Trinity's mother? He's never mentioned either of his parents."

"Deeantha, the Rainbow Runner."

That *did* startle me.

Deeantha was one of the most famous of the Ante-Fae. She was almost elemental in nature, tied to the rainbows, and she brought with her joy and light everywhere she went. She usually followed the storms of life—both actual storms and metaphorical storms, bringing relief with her. Deeantha wasn't the type to settle down. She crossed the world, running from rainbow to rainbow, braving the lightning storms as she stood at the top of the arc of the rainbows, arms stretched wide, willing the clouds to part. In a sense, she was almost a goddess among the Ante-Fae. The thought that Trinity was her son blew my mind.

"Okay. That explains a few things. He's never mentioned his family at all."

"Perhaps that's because his mother kicked him out when he was barely grown and his father wanted nothing to do with him. All Maximus cared about was having his way with Deeantha. I'm afraid Trinity got caught in the crossfire. As I said, I like Trinity, and I understand him. But he's chaotic by nature, and I don't think he's decided whether to follow the path of his father or his mother yet. But Trinity knows his origins, and I think he resents both of his parents, as well he should. So perhaps he'll just make his own way in the world, as he seems to be doing now. I just don't want you getting hurt if he should suddenly start harkening to his father's blood. Trinity does like you, I know that. I just don't ever want him getting obsessed with you. He has the capability for it."

That gave me a lot to think about. Part of me wanted to protest that Trinity was his own person, and he didn't have to follow either his mother or father. But I also knew how with the Ante-Fae, including me, parental blood played a huge part in what we ended up becoming. I was a priestess of Arawn and Cerridwen because my mother was one of the Bean Sidhe, and because my father was one of the Black Dogs. I could no more devote myself to a goddess of springtime and joy than I could peel the birthmarks off my body.

"Are you all right?" Herne asked after a moment.

I shrugged. "Yeah, I suppose I am. I just wasn't expecting that. I thought maybe Trinity had done something, but I never realized the warnings came because of who he is. I have a lot to think about. I don't want to evict him from my life just because of his bloodline. That just seems wrong. But I understand what you mean about wondering which path he'll follow. The Ante-Fae are products of our heritage, perhaps more than any of the other races. I think even more than the gods," I said, glancing at him.

Herne nodded. "I think you're right. I'd say the only other beings who follow their heritage even more than the Ante-Fae are the Luo'henkah. The elemental spirits. Sometimes I think you Ante-Fae are actually closer in nature to them than you are to the Fae themselves."

"I'm not going argue on that one either. Thank you. It actually helps me understand Trinity a lot better. I won't tell him that you told me."

Herne let out a sigh as he turned into his driveway. "I just don't want you being disappointed if he ends up being...someone you didn't expect him to be."

I laughed, shaking my head at him. "If you knew how many times crap like this has happened to me, you'd understand that I can handle disappointment. I hope I'm not taken by surprise either, but if I am, I can deal with it now that I've been forewarned." And with that, I got out of the car and straightened my skirt.

HERNE LED me around the side of his house, and past a chain-link fence that divided his yard from the park. He glanced back at my shoes.

"Are you going to be able to walk through the woods in those?"

I glanced down at my ballerina flats. "They'll be fine. And they're inexpensive enough that if I have to buy a new pair, it's no great loss."

"What about that top? Your arms are open to being scratched up as we—"

I stopped him right there. "Stop worrying about me, okay? I often go out in the woods dressed just like this. I'm pretty resilient, Herne. I know you mean well, but I don't need to be dressed up in jeans and a sweater to manage a walk in the woods. Especially since you said it wasn't far from your house. Unless your definition of far is different than mine?"

He grinned and shook his head. "I'm sorry. I just... Kipa threatened to wring my neck if you got hurt, and normally I'd give him a thrashing for that, but in this case, I understand. As to definitions, no, mine isn't different than yours. It's about five minutes up this trail and then another five minutes to the left. I was just worried about any stinging nettle that might hit you. It doesn't bother me, but it plays havoc with a lot of humans and a number of the Fae as well."

I shrugged. "Stinging nettle doesn't bother me either.

The Ante-Fae have a lot more resistance than the Fae do, at least for most things. So why didn't they put the portal in your backyard? You own your house, don't you?" I wasn't sure if he was renting or if he owned his home, but somehow it seemed like the gods wouldn't make for good renters. Although Kipa made an exception to the rule. He rented a house up in North Seattle, actually halfway around Lake Washington.

"Yes, I own it. I bought it not long ago. For a while I wasn't sure that it was a good fit for me, but it's grown on me, and Ember likes it."

I raised my eyebrows. "Do you think you're ever going to ask Ember to marry you?" I knew it was an impudent question, but I didn't think he'd mind. At worst, he would blow it off and not answer me. But to my surprise, he gave me a long look, almost puzzled.

"I thought surely…" He paused, and I saw hesitation in his eyes.

Oh gods, I had put my foot in it. "You already have, haven't you? And she hasn't given you an answer yet, has she?"

He blushed and I knew I was right. I also knew that I had to somehow smooth over the conversation before it started nagging on him. Chances were good that Ember wasn't ready yet and I didn't want to make matters tense between them.

"You do know that it takes women a while to think about it? Especially when it entails such a huge change in life style." I stopped on the pathway, my hands on my hips. "I hope you realize just how much she loves you."

He let out a long sigh, the breath whistling between his teeth. "I have to admit, it's been over a month since I asked her and she hasn't given me an answer yet. I've been nervous—did I ask too quickly? Does she even want to marry me? Is my life just too much baggage for her to take on? She knows what it entails, and you're right, it's a huge step. For one thing, she'd have to become a goddess, like my mother. It's fine for me to have a mortal girlfriend, but when it comes to marriage, the woman I offer my life must become immortal." He pulled his face, shaking his head. "I probably shouldn't have asked her this soon. We've been together for a year and I thought surely she knew how I felt—"

I could see he was working himself into a lather. I walked over to his side and grabbed his hands in mine, squeezing them tightly.

"Stop. *Just stop.* Ember loves you. You know that in your heart, and everybody who knows her knows that. When you guys are together you practically glow. And I know she trusts you, and that's incredibly important to women. She'll give you her answer when she's thought it through. And my guess is that she'll say yes. I don't know for sure, but I do know Ember, and I know how much she cares about you and how much she loves you. Just give her time to work through all the ramifications. And then when she does answer, she'll have no hesitation."

He gazed down at me, his eyes piercing and yet gentle. I could almost see the stag behind those glacial pools of blue. I could feel the Wild Hunt within him, coursing through his blood. It reminded me of when I felt the wolves racing within Kipa, the high crags and snowy mountains that he so loved. They were two of a kind, now that I thought of it. Herne and his cousin Kipa were two sides of a coin, summer and winter, oak and holly. And

Ember and I were just lucky enough to each hold one side of the coin in our heart.

"Thank you," Herne said. "Thank you for saying that. And I know you mean it, and I know Ember loves me. You're right, she'll give me her answer when she's ready and I can wait until then. I won't push her and I won't rush her."

"Good, because that is the worst thing you could do. All right, let's get on with this. Ferosyn's waiting for me." Giving Herne a final smile, I let his hands drop and stood back. He took up the lead again and we headed up the trail, and then to the left on a side trail that led to a clearing not far beyond.

Twin oaks stood in the clearing, huge and magnificent, sentinels over the rest of the park. There was a crackling energy between them, and I could feel the essence of the portal reaching out. It was like a web drawn between the trees, a network of scintillating threads, snapping and crackling as they created a vortex.

The portal keeper was there, and he gave Herne a nod.

"Everything's ready for you, Lord Herne."

"Thank you. We'll be back later on this evening, or at least Raven will. This is set for my father's palace?"

The portal keeper nodded, and stood back. Herne turned to me and held out his hand.

"Take my hand if you like. I'm not sure how often you've traveled through the portals. They can be quite disconcerting if you're not used to them."

"Oh, I'm fine. But thank you, anyway. I think it might steady me, now that you mention it." I placed my fingers in his, and with him holding my hand firmly, we stepped between the oaks, into the portal, and in a flash we transported to Annwn.

SUMMER IN ANNWN WAS BEAUTIFUL. We came out not far from Cernunnos's Palace. The portal keeper there waved us onto the path, bowing as Herne passed by. The keeper was an Elf, as were most of the people bustling by. It looked to be an active day, and I glanced down the road when I caught sight of the marketplace. I wanted to go explore, but we didn't have time.

"Is that a bazaar?" I asked, pointing toward the market.

Herne nodded. "Yes, it's actually the Eselwithe bazaar, and it's open every day from sunup to sundown. You'll find vendors of all sorts there."

"Is Eselwithe a village?" I wasn't too clear on how things worked over here in Annwn.

"Yes, it's actually the village that surrounds my father's palace. Mostly Elves live there, although a few Fae make their homes there as well. Someday I mean to bring Ember over here and stay for a week so she can explore the area." He looked around, a gentle smile on his face, and I realized he was glad to be home.

"You love it here, don't you?"

"Does it show that much?" he asked. "I do love it here. And I miss being over here more. I've lived over on Earth for so many years now, but every now and then I take a few months and come back here. Now and then I've taken a year or two, but not since I moved to the United States. It seems like my duties with the Wild Hunt have grown more perilous as the days have gone on. Some days, I wish I could just hand it off to somebody else and return here for good. But I think I'd miss my home there too."

"You've acclimated and now you've essentially got dual citizenship in your heart."

He glanced at me, a sad look on his face. "Yes. I'm torn between worlds. I love *both* my homes, and I'm not sure if I was forced to choose which side I would return to." He paused, then added, "You're easy to talk to, Raven, and that's a compliment. I don't know why, but I find myself telling you things I haven't even told Ember yet."

"Perhaps because you don't have as much to lose when you're talking to me. If you tell her something that makes her upset or question your relationship, there are severe ramifications. If *I* question what you say, it doesn't matter so much. That's why. But I think you should talk to Ember about some of this. I think she needs to know how you feel."

We backed away as a cart trundled past, the back of it heaped with vegetables and large bottles of what looked like milk. I frowned, leaning closer.

"Hey, aren't those bottles made by the Johnson Company? From Earth?"

He laughed then, slapping his thigh. "It's not like there isn't any commerce between the two realms. There are some things that humans do better than the Elves." And with that, he motioned for me to follow him and we headed up the slope leading to the great tree palace of Cernunnos.

FEROSYN WAS WAITING for me when Herne led me into the Healing Center.

Set toward the back of Cernunnos's Palace, the Healing Center was a multilevel complex. The entire palace was built in a tree, which had originally startled me when I was first brought over to heal up from what Pandora did to me. But it made sense.

Cernunnos was Lord of the Forest, and it stood to reason that he would live in a massive treehouse that spanned several giant oaks. And by giant, I meant *massive*. The trees were easily double and triple the size of the biggest oaks over on Earth, rising hundreds of feet into the air and spreading across massive areas of the woodland.

Manned mostly by Elves, the palace was a testament to the power of Herne's father. Everywhere, series of staircases led from one tree to another, and rope elevators, their cars built from lightweight wood, offered access to those who had trouble walking.

The Healing Center was in a separate tree than the main palace, although Ferosyn often worked out of an infirmary located near the throne room. Herne led me over to one of the elevators and I cocked my head, looking first at the wooden car, then at Herne.

"I can climb stairs, if you'd rather."

He shook his head. "The Healing Center is at the top of the tree. There would be a lot of stairs to climb between here and there, and if we want to make your appointment, we better go as quickly as we can." He opened the car door and I stepped inside, feeling slightly squeamish. I wasn't afraid of heights, but the ropes looked so lightweight, and the distance to the platform to which we were heading was so far up that it made me nervous. Herne noticed my concern and was quick to reassure me.

"These ropes are made by the Elves, and they'll support thousands of pounds—far more than we could fit inside this car. And the pulley systems are checked every morning and every evening. We'll be safe."

I let out a sigh of relief. "Thank you. I guess I'm not doing too well at covering up my feelings lately."

"I don't think you should try," Herne said. "Repressing your feelings is never really a good thing. Well, I can think of a few exceptions, but over something like being nervous about an elevator ride? Not necessary." He grinned at me.

"I see why Ember loves you so much. You're so supportive, and I hope you realize how much I appreciate it. It's been a rough past couple months."

He regarded me carefully for a moment, then said, "May I ask how you and Kipa are doing?"

It was my turn to smile. "We've had a bit of a rough patch lately, mostly due to me trying to deal with all of this and keep him safe from worrying about me. But Kipa's a rock, he's my anchor. I think you underestimate him, Herne. I haven't known him for a long time, and I know you have history with him that hasn't been pleasant, but don't underestimate him." I paused, wanting to tell him that Nya had been the one to initiate the tryst with Kipa, but since Kipa had kept it a secret, I would too. But I swore to myself that if Herne ever brought it up, if he ever threw it at Kipa when I was around, I wouldn't keep quiet.

Herne stared over the side of the car as we ascended through the tree limbs. "Perhaps you're right. He does seem to have changed for the better. I'm glad that you get

along with him. I just… I just don't want to see you hurt."
He gnawed on his lip, giving me a sideways glance.

"Kipa told me he loved me the other night. And I said
it back. I don't know where we're going, or how long it
will last, but even though I'm a lot younger than you, I do
know my own mind. I was engaged for a long time to
someone I loved, and I lost him. But I have to tell you this:
I never loved Ulstair the way I love Kipa. Ulstair and I got
along, we fit together in so many ways. Don't get me
wrong, I would have married him if he was still alive…
one day. But I didn't have the same passion that I do for
your cousin. Ulstair couldn't match me the way Kipa
does. He was too easy for me, and I think I was too hard
for him. I value your friendship very much. But I'd rather
have you as a buddy than a big brother."

Herne gave me a little shrug. "Heard and registered. I
won't try to dissuade you again."

At that moment, the wooden elevator car came to a
stop and Herne locked it into place before opening the
gate. We exited onto a ledge near a door, so far up in the
tree I could barely see the ground. A circular staircase
wound around the massive trunk, descending toward the
ground. The hand-carved railing ensured that no one
could fall off. There were two doors in front of us, leading
into the tree, and over the doors was a sign that I couldn't
read.

"What language is that?"

"Elvish. It reads 'Healing Center.' " And with that,
Herne opened the door to escort me in, and I ducked
inside as a light rain began to fall, sprinkling down
through the leaves.

CHAPTER ELEVEN

UNLIKE ALL THE COMPLAINTS I HEARD ABOUT HUMAN doctors, Ferosyn didn't make me wait more than a couple minutes before he ushered me into his office. Herne went off to meet his father, and told me that Ferosyn would provide me with someone to take me back to the portal when I was ready to go home. He made sure I had enough money for an LUD ride back to my house.

Ferosyn looked as young as I did, but I knew he was thousands of years older. The Elves lived almost as long as the gods, even longer than most of the Fae. I wasn't sure how they compared in relationship with the Ante-Fae, but I figured it couldn't be much different. The Ante-Fae outlived the Fae by centuries—even millennia in some cases, but I still had a feeling the Elves had us beat in longevity.

"Have a seat, Raven." Ferosyn sat down behind his desk, which was made of a polished mahogany. The wood reverberated with energy and I realize that everything within the halls of Cernunnos's palace was alive in its own right.

I sat on the velvet divan opposite, feeling distinctly uncomfortable. I fidgeted with my purse, before answering. "Hey, so I'm back."

Healers among the communities over in Annwn weren't called "doctor," like over on Earth. Often they were addressed with the title "healer" in front of their name, but Ferosyn never seem to stand on ceremony. In general, I was comfortable around him, but right now, I felt like I was walking on eggshells.

"Herne says that you're interested in talking to one of our therapists?" There was no accusation in his voice, and no judgment, just a simple question.

I nodded, looking up to meet his gaze. "I'm having some problems. I really thought I could manage this on my own. I thought I was strong enough, but I'm having flashbacks, and the memories are interfering with my relationships and actually just screwing up my ability to function."

"Post-traumatic stress disorder affects more than just humans, Raven. I'd be surprised if you weren't affected by this. I'd actually be worried."

"Worried?" That seemed strange to me.

"Yes, worried, because it would mean that you were repressing your feelings. You know Rafé came here for help?"

I nodded. "He said you guys helped a lot."

"We did, but we can only help when someone's ready to accept it. And asking for help is the first step. There's absolutely nothing we can do for anyone who isn't willing to admit that they need assistance. So I'm glad to hear you ask, because it means you're ready to truly heal and let go." He smiled, sitting back in his chair.

"Isn't there a pill you could give me? Or some herbs that would just wipe it all away?"

"I'm afraid it doesn't work like that, not even with magic. No, I think I should pair you up with Sejun. I think you'll do better with him than you would with a woman, considering it was a woman who traumatized you."

That made sense to me. "So, when do I start? And do I have to come over to Annwn every time I need to talk to him?"

Ferosyn shook his head. "No, Sejun can come to your house. I want to start you at twice a week, for about two hours each time. That's an intensive amount of therapy to put in, but I think that you will respond well to it. And I think you'll be more comfortable talking in your own home."

Feeling relieved, I let out a long breath. "Yeah, actually I would. So do I start today?"

"I think that's the best thing, don't you? There's no sense in waiting. You'll have your first session here, and then Sejun will take you back over to Earth, where he will escort you to your home so he knows where to go. If you have any trouble at all, just let me know. We have a number of healers and therapists and I can pair you with someone else if it doesn't work out."

Hoping that I wouldn't have to worry about that, I simply nodded. "What do I owe you?"

"I'm on retainer," Ferosyn said. "Cernunnos pays me more than I actually need." He reached up and rang a bell next to his desk. A woman whom I assumed was a nurse entered the room, dressed in a calf-length white gown, her hair tightly braided back and hanging down to her waist. She was beautiful, an Elf, but she looked older than Ferosyn himself. I wondered how long she'd been around, but decided that would be rude to ask.

"Mesaue Fortunlea, would you please escort Ms. BoneTalker to Sejun's office? Thank you," Ferosyn said.

The nurse nodded to him, then motioned for me to follow her. We headed down a corridor door that was brightly lit. The floor here appeared to be marble, and the walls were textured wood, but they were painted a light white color, with just a hint of pale green. They were easy on the eyes, and made me feel oddly calm. We turned two or three times along the way into other hallways until we came to a door. She tapped on it, then entered, motioning for me to follow her.

The office reminded me of a medical office over on Earth, except it felt more soothing, and there was even an aquarium here. I shook my head, laughing.

"Did you get that over on Earth?" I asked.

Mesaue Fortunlea smiled, her somber demeanor dropping away. "Yes, and it is Sejun's pride and joy. He loves those fish so much."

I bent over to examine the fish while she tapped on an inner door, then peeked inside to murmur something I couldn't quite hear. The fish were darting around, looking extremely energetic for fish, and one came up to the side of the aquarium, watching me through the glass.

"Ms. BoneTalker? You may go in. Sejun is waiting for you."

As she held the inner door open for me, I felt oddly reluctant. Walking through that door was to admit that I couldn't handle this myself, and I hated that thought. But it was true, I couldn't. So taking a deep breath, I entered the room, deciding to place my mental health in a stranger's hands.

By THE TIME Sejun and I left his office, I was reeling and I wasn't sure why. It wasn't like we had talked over anything that seemed incredibly difficult, but somehow, he seemed to draw the trauma up to the surface, and to start skimming it off of me. I had told him what happened, not in terrible detail, and I hadn't even talked about how painful it had been. But I felt like a scab had been ripped off and I was open and raw. He had given me a bottle of herbal capsules, and instructed me to take one before bedtime.

"It will help you sleep and heal. Come now, I'll escort you home. I'll see you on Saturday, at three P.M. your time." He was very professional, but the moment we left his office, he seemed to relax and totally veered away from the subject of my visit.

"Do you like living among humans? I've never had much interaction with them," the Elf said.

"Yeah, I do. But I'm one of the Exosan—the Ante-Fae who tend to hang out with humans. We're all younger, most of us well under five hundred years old. The older generations don't tend to understand what we see about interacting with humankind or with the Fae. But they're our descendants—the Fae are—and it just makes sense to form some sort of connection. And humans cover the planet. It doesn't seem like a wise move to just ignore their existence." I paused as we got into the elevator car again. Holding onto the railing, I closed my eyes so I wouldn't see our descent.

"Afraid of heights?"

"No, not terribly, but this seems like such a flimsy contraption. Even though Herne reassured me that it was safe, I still don't feel that confident about it." I tried to laugh off my nerves, but the truth was that when we reached the bottom, I took a huge breath of relief.

"Not to insult your engineers, but I think I prefer the elevators over where I come from." I looked around, as the street seemed to be emptying. The sun was headed toward the horizon, and it seemed cooler over here than it did back home.

"People are going home for the day. The bazaar shuts down around this time each night, and earlier in winter." Sejun crooked his arm, waiting. I realized he meant for me to slide my arm through his so he could escort me properly. Feeling odd, but not wanting to insult him, I obliged.

He motioned for a carriage, and before I could say a word, we were bundled inside, heading toward the portal. Sejun didn't talk much, but that didn't surprise me. Most Elves weren't very talkative. Instead, I looked out the window, watching as people wandered along the road toward the village of Eselwithe. Rows of houses were lit from within, and smoke rose into the air from the chimneys. It seemed odd to look up and see the glimmer of stars appearing in the sky already. But there was no light pollution here to block them out, and because of that, it seemed that night fell faster here.

"What are you looking at?" Sejun asked.

"The sky. We see the stars over where I come from, but

not nearly so clear. Here there's nothing to block their light. I think I'd like to come back here and go camping sometime. Maybe Kipa can bring me." I realized that I really did want that. While I wasn't exactly the camping sort of girl, I did enjoy spending time in the forest. And it would be nice to get away, just Kipa and Raj and me.

"I think you should do it. I think you'd enjoy that a lot from what you told me about yourself." He paused, then added, "Don't forget to take those capsules at night. One per night. They'll help get you through the rough parts of therapy, and sleep will help you heal. My guess is that your sleep is been highly interrupted for the past few weeks, am I right?"

I nodded. "You don't know how right you are. I haven't had a good night's sleep in weeks. I wake up at the slightest sound, and when I do sleep I have either night-mares or confusing dreams that I don't understand but that leave me feeling uneasy and out of sorts."

"I think tonight will be a little bit easier." Sejun stopped, looking back out the window. A few minutes later we pulled in toward the portal, and he got out, holding up his hand to help me down from the carriage. I gave him a quick curtsey and then we sauntered over toward the twin oaks.

He talked to the portal keeper for a moment, then motioned to me and held out his hand.

"Once we get over there, you'll have to take the lead. I'll be out of my element. But it will do me good. I haven't been over that way in a long time, and it will remind me of just what environment you're coming from. Plus I'll have to get used to it, coming over twice a week for a while."

I bit my lip." How long do you think it's going to take for me to get over this?"

"I don't know if you ever get over something like that, but if you're asking how long will it take you to feel back to normal? Probably less time than you expect." Then, giving my hand a quick squeeze, he walked toward the portal and I followed. Hand in hand, we stepped through the oaks, back into Seattle.

THE PORTAL KEEPER was waiting there. "Herne asked me to drive you down to the parking garage to pick up your car."

"That works for me. Then, after I show Sejun where I live, I'll send him back in an LUD. I'll call to schedule a ride right now. They take reservations. I'll put his fare on my credit card." I scrambled into the back of the car, and Sejun followed, looking slightly uncomfortable.

It suddenly occurred to me that I didn't remember much about what we discussed during the actual session. It was almost as if the entire appointment had been a dream that was quickly slipping away. I was going to say something, then decided that it wasn't anything to worry about. After we picked up my Subaru, we headed across the 520 floating bridge over to the Eastside.

As we stepped out of the car at my home, Sejun looked around, giving a nod of approval. "You have a very nice home," he said. "How long have you lived here?"

"Oh, a number of years. My father helped me buy the place. Did you want to come in for a drink or something?"

But as I spoke, the LUD drove up, right on time. "Oh, there's your ride. We can reschedule it, if you like."

He shook his head. "No, I'd best be getting home. I have a photographic memory. Now that I know your address, and the route, I'll be able to find my way here no matter what portal I come through. I'll see you on Saturday at three. Until then, remember—"

"Take the capsules, one per night. I'll remember. And Sejun, thank you. I appreciate your help. I don't know how the treatments will work for me, but I have an open mind and I'm hopeful."

"That's all I can ask for," he said, heading back to the LUD. As I watched the car drive off into the street, I realized that I really *didn't* remember anything we had talked about. Feeling slightly confused, but lighter of heart, I unlocked the door and entered the house.

Kipa wasn't home yet, but the wards were still set and the security system hadn't been tampered with. After setting down my purse and keys, I looked around for Raj. He was nowhere in sight and a momentary panic crept over me.

"Raj? Raj? Where are you?" It wasn't like Raj to hide when I got home. I peeked in my office but he wasn't there. He hadn't been in the living room and I didn't notice him in the kitchen when I passed by. Starting to fear that he had somehow found his way outside and ended up lost, I dashed down the hall to my bedroom and peeked around the corner.

There he was, sitting on my bed, wearing one of my

bathrobes. Sometimes Raj liked to play dress-up, which I found odd given that gargoyles generally went around naked.

"Raj scared Raven! Raven thought Raj had gone outside by himself. What's Raj doing?" I asked, heading toward the bed.

"Raj isn't doing anything," came the reply. He stared at me blankly, his go-to "I didn't do anything" look.

I hadn't forbade him to play dress-up, but he was rough on my clothes and so I had bought him some thrift-store garb. He knew he wasn't supposed to use my clothes instead.

"Why is Raj wearing Raven's bathrobe?"

He glanced the other way, trying to avoid my eyes. "What bathrobe? Raj doesn't see any bathrobe."

"Raj knows *perfectly well* that Raven can see that he's wearing her bathrobe. Raj also knows that Raven won't be angry, unless Raj lies to her or does something he's not supposed to. Now did Raven say Raj can wear her bathrobe?"

Raj thought for a moment, then shook his head. "No. Raven said Raj must wear his own clothes."

"Then Raj needs to tell Raven the truth." With a sigh, I sprawled on the bed, staring at the ceiling as I folded my arms under my head. "Why is Raj wearing Raven's bathrobe?"

Raj deflated. He slipped out of the bathrobe, trying to fold it but only ended up ripping it in the process. I grimaced. The purple satin was one of my favorites, but I didn't want to yell at him. He hadn't meant to tear it.

"Raj missed Raven. Raj was pretending Raven was here to talk to him."

Oh, good gods. Had I gotten that bad? I knew that I'd been distant lately, but I tried to be present as much as I could. However, Raj wasn't like a happy-go-lucky dog who could handle a couple weeks of vacation if their owner left town. Raj was more like an extremely neurotic cat, and he acted out just like one.

"Raven hasn't been too far from home most of the time lately," I said, sitting up and folding my knees into a cross-legged position.

"Raj knows. But it feels like Raven's been gone. Raven seems distant to Raj. Raj wonders what he did to drive Raven away." He looked so forlorn that I burst into tears. The day had been exhausting, even though I couldn't remember part of it. "Now Raj makes Raven cry."

I scooted up toward the headboard and patted the pillow next me as I leaned back. "Raj come sit with Raven." As the massive gargoyle half-rolled, half-crawled his way up the bed, I laid my arm out wide and Raj slipped inside of my embrace, leaning against me with a contented sigh.

"So, Raj should tell Raven just how he's feeling right now."

Raj paused, then he closed his eyes and leaned against my side. "Raj is nervous. Raj is worried about Raven. She seems different and sad. Raj is worried that Raven's going to go away and leave him alone."

So *that* was it. He was afraid I was going to abandon him. I leaned down and kissed the top of his head.

"Oh Raj, *please* don't worry about that. Raven's not going anywhere, and if she does, she'll take Raj with her. Raj and Raven are a *team*, and Raj, Raven, and Kipa are a team. And what do teams do?"

"Teams work together. Rah-rah!" He waved one hand in the air, trying to clumsily give me a high five. I high-fived him back, and then tickled his belly. It was the softest place on him, a small spot on his underbelly. Like the dragons and Shelob of Tolkien, that was his most vulnerable place. He laughed and the sparkle started coming back into his eyes.

"Raven promise?" Raj giggled in between his words, then fell into that nasal laugh of his. The smile on his face told me everything I needed to know.

"Raven promises. And you know Raven never breaks a promise if she can help it."

At that moment, I heard the front door open. I stiffened, but then Kipa called from the living room.

"I'm home! Where are you?"

"Raj and I are in the bedroom. Come on in."

Kipa entered the bedroom, holding a bouquet of roses and a can of very fancy cat food. "Roses for my Raven, and Sheer Perfection for Raj."

Raj rolled onto his back, wriggling.

I rose up on my knees, accepting the flowers as Kipa leaned down to give me a kiss. I scooted over, patting the bed next to me. "Sit down. These are beautiful," I said, pressing my nose to the blossoms.

They were fuchsia, brilliant pink with darker pink edges. And they smelled like a wild garden, like a secret garden at night. I thought back to the place over near the veterans' home, shivering. But these roses hadn't come from there, and their spicy scent swept my thoughts away from ghosts and monsters. I set them aside and leaned over to kiss Kipa. He pulled me into his arms, and I strad-dled his lap, wrapping my legs around his waist. I was hungry for him, suddenly wanting him more than I had wanted anything for a long time. I caught my breath, gazing into his eyes, resting my head against his.

"Raj, would you like to go eat your dinner?" I asked.

Raj jumped off the bed, dropping the can of cat food in his excitement. Kipa glanced at me and I nodded.

"Come on, Raj, I'll feed you your dinner a little early." Kipa turned back to me as he scooped up the can of cat food. "Get ready for me," he said as he darted out the door with Raj following.

CHAPTER TWELVE

I HAD STRIPPED DOWN AND WAS STARTING TO PUT ON A sheer black negligée when Kipa burst into the room. Only he didn't look turned on. Instead, there was a worried expression across his face.

"I just got a call from Herne. He wants to know if you can come help us out." He froze, looking me up and down. "*Damn*, you look hot."

My libido took a nosedive. "What's happening now?"

"I think you really *did* wake something up. Up at the Worchester cemetery, reports have come in that there are some skeletal walkers on the move." He shrugged. "Herne could call somebody else, but you're the quickest bone witch or necromancer to reach. You know how to deal with the dead—and the undead."

"Crap. Okay, call him back and tell him we're on the way. I'll get dressed."

As Kipa darted out of my room, I pulled off the night-gown and rummaged through my dresser, grabbing a pair of black-and-white striped leggings, which I shimmied into. I pulled a black jersey tank dress over my head and fitted a silver belt around the waist. Then I slid into a pair of black Fluevog Socas. I pulled my hair back into a ponytail and slid a lightweight black denim jacket over the top. I slung my purse over my shoulder, and quickly stopped in my ritual room to grab my bag of tricks.

Kipa was waiting by the door. He had already explained to Raj that we were going to have to go out. I noticed that he had armed the wards, and the security system. We hustled out to the car and I tossed him the keys.

"I want to do some meditation and start building energy for spell work."

I jammed my seatbelt on as Kipa pulled out of the driveway and we sped up the road. He was a good driver, if a little bit reckless, but he had never gotten a ticket and he had never hurt anybody.

I leaned back in my seat, closing my eyes. "You said skeletal walkers?"

Skeletal walkers were different than zombies or ghouls. Reanimated bones, they had no sense or thought. Brainless, they merely carried out the orders their keeper programmed into them. The problem was, they wouldn't stop until they were destroyed—as in pulverized. Skeletal walkers didn't attack out of hunger or fear, and not once had I ever seen one spontaneously reanimate. No, they had to be given orders by either a necromancer or someone who worked with the dead. Given the conditions, I rather doubted that the Lykren was to blame for this. From what we had read, the Lykren couldn't command the dead. No, there was someone else behind this.

I drifted in the energy, gathering my power around me. Those of us who worked magic at the level I did could handle potent spells, but we had a limited amount of juice to go on. And when we were tired, the amount of magical energy we had to spare diminished accordingly. Strong emotions, physical exertion, lack of sleep—all of these factors played a part in how much magic we could perform, as well as how strong the spells we could cast.

And right now I wasn't feeling incredibly strong. *However*, I was still horny, and I could use that as a substitute. Sexual energy and magical energy were close together in terms of both source and strength, tied through the kundalini channels. And so, I channeled my arousal into my magic, focusing on strengthening the magical nature of the energy. It was a little bit like sorting different-colored M&Ms. Right now I was setting the green ones to the side, and keeping the orange and red ones for myself. And yet, the fact that there *were* green ones meant there were also more red and orange to go around.

Ten minutes later, I was breathing easy, my frustration gone. My strength felt like it was returning. I let out a long breath and opened my eyes.

Kipa glanced over at me, a knowing look on his face. "You're ready to go on the attack, aren't you?"

I nodded. "Yes, I can manage a fight against the skeletal walkers tonight." I paused, then reached forward and opened my glove box to grab a couple candy bars that I kept there. The sugar would give me another temporary energy boost. I ate one of the Shasta bars, and then the other. They were coconut and chocolate, with cherry flavoring added in.

"I don't know how you can eat those things," Kipa said with a laugh. "Give me a good old-fashioned chocolate bar any day without anything in it but a few nuts."

"I'm pretty sure we can manage to find the nuts. They seem to be breeding pretty fast these days. The chocolate I'm not so sure about," I said with a laugh. "I like Shasta bars. I especially like the peanut butter ones." I licked my fingers, then hunted in my purse for a wet wipe. As I wiped my hands, I added, "I saw one of the therapists at Ferosyn's today. His name is Sejun. He gave me some herbal capsules for bedtime, to help me sleep better."

"How do you feel about going to therapy, now that you've been?" Kipa asked, swinging the car onto the 520 floating bridge. Traffic was light, given rush hour was over, and the brightness of Seattle glittered across the lake. Lake Washington was beautiful, stretching for miles either way. Twenty-two miles lengthways, the lake supported the floating bridge, which in itself was over a mile across, stretching from the Eastside to Seattle proper. During storms, the water frothed at the edges, sweeping over the pontoons.

"I think it's going to be good, although it's the strangest thing. I can't remember anything that happened during the session. I can't remember what I told him, I can't remember what he said. I just have a feeling that whatever it was, it was helpful." I realized that I did feel a bit lighter, a little less weighed down.

"Do you realize how the therapists there work? Especially with traumatic cases?"

I shook my head. "I have no idea."

"I'm not sure if I'm supposed to tell you, but I feel you should know. They bring the trauma to the surface while you're talking to them, and then… They sort of *absorb* it out of your system. Then they cleanse it and let it go. They actually *remove* the traumatic injury to the psyche."

I stared at him, my jaw dropping. "They do *what?*"

"Yes. Sejun's actually siphoning the energy of the wound off of you and releasing it. You'll keep the memories of what happened, but pretty soon they shouldn't bother you—or at least, they won't be painful flashbacks." Kipa frowned, looking worried. "Should I have kept my mouth shut?"

I wasn't sure what to say. The idea that someone was siphoning off my pain felt both invasive and yet incredibly freeing. I didn't know how I felt about it.

"I'm going to have to process that for a while. I'm glad you told me. Herne didn't say anything and neither did Ferosyn. You know, it would be so helpful if humans could devise a similar sort of treatment. There are some pretty broken people out there."

"I know," Kipa said. "Venla had some dark secrets of her own when I was with her. I couldn't help her that way, but at least I had love to offer, and a safe haven for the rest of her life." His voice was tender, and I realized it sounded the same as when he was being gentle with me.

"You really did love her, didn't you?" I looked at him, watching his expression.

He kept his eyes on the road, but gave me a nod. "I did. People wonder how the gods can love humans, but love transcends so many factors. Obstacles crumble in the face of it. I loved Venla in a way that I had never loved anyone. And in a way I've never loved anyone since… Until now." He pressed his lips together, focusing on driving.

I leaned back in my seat again, thinking about everything he told me. "I think, as long as Sejun leaves all my other feelings and emotions alone, I'm glad that he's doing what he's doing. I hate the fact that I don't trust myself right now. I want to blame Pandora and not my own bad judgment, but it's hard for me to do that, given I gave her a ride in the middle of the night, only having met her briefly."

"Everything she did to you is her fault, and her fault alone. You are not to blame for what happened to you, Raven. You're never to blame for that. And one day, I will pay Pandora a visit, and I'll make sure she understands why she should never mess with my loved ones again. I give you my oath. Because like Pandora, I'm a god, and I can do some serious damage to her. And that's all we'll say about that for now."

We drove in silence toward the Worchester District. I ran through my repertoire of spells that dealt with the undead, especially with skeletal walkers. There were several that could turn them to dust, but I didn't know if I had enough energy for that. But I could freeze them in place until somebody else could beat the crap out of them. Once the bones were ground to dust, the magic would vanish. But they had to be pulverized, or the hands could creep around and still wreak havoc. That was where the story of the monkey's paw originated.

As we came to the cemetery, I straightened up and hid my purse under the seat, stowing my phone and my keys in my pockets. Kipa had brought out a large wooden hammer, given blunt instruments worked better against skeletons than swords, and we pulled into the parking lot, where I recognized Herne's car and Ember's car. As we stepped out onto the sidewalk, I could see Herne and Ember at a distance, keeping an eye on several creatures that were headed their way. Viktor stood near his car, and I waved to him.

"Are you ready to bust some ass?" I asked.

"You've got it, chickadee!" he said, swinging a large hammer that he had propped over his shoulder. Actually, it was more like a giant croquet mallet, only it had metal ends on either side, and the wood looked to be a whole lot sturdier than whatever they used for the game. "So, do you think the Lykren stirred this up?"

I shook my head as we hurried over to him. "No. The Lykren can't animate the dead. This is somebody else's work." At that moment my phone rang, and I glanced at the caller ID. It was Ashera. That was a surprise.

Ashera also had a big hand in helping me escape from Pandora. One of the Dragonni, she was a blue dragon shifter who did *not* share the destructive tendencies of Typhon, the Father of Dragons. When the Dragonni began to return to this world, Ashera had been one of them. She now lived on Bainbridge Island, to be near the water. We knew that there were several other dragons around, including twin white dragons who were Pandora's helpers.

"Ashera, what can I do for you?" I was pleased to hear from her, even considering the circumstances.

"I wanted to tell you that Aso and Variance have been spotted in the Seattle area. I'm not sure what they're up to, but they came down off the mountain. One of my informants saw them and gave me a call."

I blinked. So Ashera already had informants? That was news. "Can they raise skeletal walkers?"

"There's not much those two *can't* do in terms of the dead. So, yes, I would assume they can."

"Can I call you back later? I'm about to go into battle with a few of the bony-assed creatures." I said good-bye and jammed my phone back in my pocket. "I think we know who animated the skeletal walkers, guys. Aso and Variance have been spotted in Seattle. It looks like they're getting ready to raise hell for their father."

"We'll talk about that later," Viktor said, swinging in beside Kipa and me. "Right now we need to send those walkers back to the grave."

And with that, we headed over to meet Ember and Herne, weapons ready.

I COULD SEE six skeletal walkers. I edged over to Ember, my gaze focused on the undead. "Do you know where they're headed? Any time anyone animates a skeleton, they usually give them specific instructions. They don't usually just let them run amok."

Ember shook her head. "I don't know. One of Talia's friends called her to tell her about them. He was walking by the cemetery when he saw them and he hurried out of here as soon as he could. He knew what they were. I wonder who animated them."

"I think I might know. I just got a call from Ashera over on Bainbridge Island. She said Aso and Variance were spotted in Seattle. Chances are they are starting something for their father. I suppose it could be payback for driving Pandora out, but I quite doubt that she has left the area."

I stepped forward, trying to gauge how far apart the skeletons were. If they stretched their arms out, they would have been able to touch the fingertips of the skeleton next to them, and they were walking in three rows of two. With my spell, I could probably freeze three to four of them, but that would leave two loose to roam free.

"Damn it, the dragons. Of course." Herne shook his head. "Just what we need. Damn Typhon's spawn."

"Okay, here's the thing," I said. "I have a spell that can freeze three of them, possibly four. But you're going to have to work fast after that because it will only hold them for possibly two or three minutes. You're going to have to beat the crap out of those creatures, and the ones who aren't affected by it will be attacking you. Unless they were given some extremely specific instructions, when you attack one of a group of skeletal walkers, the others will turn on you. They often act with a hive mind—or rather, a mindless hive acting on orders as one unit. They aren't reasoning beings, and they have no needs of their own, like ghouls or zombies. Tell me when you want me to cast the spell, because it's the best one I've got for the situation."

Herne nodded, pointing to Viktor and Kipa. "I suggest that when Raven casts the spell the three of us go in and break apart the ones who are still unaffected. Then we can go to work on the ones that are being held. Ember, protect Raven. Raven, do you need to concentrate on the spell during the entire time that it's working?"

I shook my head. "No, this is one I can just cast and let go. But once I'm done with that, there's not going to be much I can do. It's an extremely potent spell, and I'm aiming for maximum effect. If I just targeted one I would have more energy."

"Okay, then Ember, definitely protect Raven. If they get through us and head toward you, the two of you run back and get in the car. I don't care which car, just get in it and lock the doors." Herne paused, glancing at me. "Can they break into cars easily?"

I shrugged. "Eventually they can break through the glass of the windows or windshield. But I think it will take them a while. Even though they are far stronger than they normally would be if they were just in their inanimate form, their bones don't weigh that much and so when they beat against the window, if it's a single pane it will break. But car glass is sturdier. Okay, they're close enough. I need space so the rest of you fan out and get ready to go."

The skeletal walkers were close enough now to see clearly. And that's exactly what they were—walking skeletons, shuffling across the lawn as their bones made rippling noises like an eerie xylophone. Their jaws were open, as if they were trying to speak but nothing came out, and no sound came out of their mouths.

A red fire glowed from their eyes, giving them sight enough to see where they were going, but it wasn't *their* sight—it was the sight of whoever had animated them. It was like a form of radar. I wasn't sure exactly how it worked, but it gave the skeletal walkers a sense of where trees and people and animals were. It didn't process through their minds, because they had no minds, but it was like a robot sensing where something was.

I summoned up my energy, gathering it up like a coiling vortex inside, and I willed it into my fingers, ready to cast as I held out my hands toward the walkers. I took a deep breath, and then in a loud voice, cast the enchantment.

> *The flesh is gone, the bone remains,*
> *no blood runs through skeletal veins,*
> *life force replaced by magic will,*
> *I now command thee, freeze, be still.*

In one great rush, the energy billowed out toward the walkers, surrounding them with a misty cloud. It blew through their eye sockets, through their gaping mouths, surrounding their bones. The walkers slowed, as though they were walking through mud and then, fully paralyzed, three of them stopped, caught in stasis until the spell wore off.

The other three kept coming, unaffected by the spell. Viktor, Kipa, and Herne moved in, swinging their great hammers. The skeletons reached out, clawing at them, but the men were able to keep them at bay as they hit the creatures again and again.

Herne let out a grunt and with one mighty swing, his skeletal opponent shattered, the bones falling apart. The magic had held them together like glue, until at last brute force broke through. Viktor managed to decapitate his skeleton, and Kipa knocked the legs out from under the one he was fighting. It went down, still clawing its way to him, using its hands to pull itself along.

Herne moved onto the frozen ones, swinging again and again.

I held my breath, hoping that the spell would keep, that it wouldn't break until they were so much dust and powder. But the next moment, Herne yelled, as one of the skeletons that had been frozen began to move again. The skeleton Kipa was fighting was still dragging itself along the ground toward him, but he swung his hammer high, bringing it down on the skull. The thick bone fractured, breaking it into pieces. Its arms were still moving, still trying to drag the torso forward, but it couldn't sense where anyone was.

Kipa turned to the other frozen skeletons who were now on the move again.

Ember tapped me on the shoulder. "We should get back."

I nodded, wondering if I had enough magic left to try for another spell, but I knew that I couldn't manage it. I let her lead me back away from the fight, which was growing closer.

The men continued to battle the skeletons, and the sound of crunching bones filled the air. The skeletons neither screamed nor wailed, nor gave any sign that they were in pain. And truly, they weren't. They were mere automatons, playthings for the Dragonni. But it was still unsettling to watch the men pulverizing these creatures who at one time had been the framework for human beings. But the body was no more the heart of the spirit than a box was the sum of what it held within it. Bodies were vessels, and so were the skeletons—simply a physical part of mortal existence.

One of the skeletons managed to latch hold of Herne's ankle—it was the headless one without legs that had been dragging itself along the ground. Herne cursed and brought his hammer down, smashing the vertebrae and the ribs, and then the arm bones. Finally, he pulled the hand bones away from his leg and tossed it across the lawn. It tried to scuttle back to him and he brought his boot down on it, shattering it into fragments until it was finally still.

I shook my head. If it took two gods and a half-ogre to fight six skeletal walkers, what would we do when Typhon was really active on this world?

I turned to Ember. "If this fight is this difficult, can you imagine if the Dragonni enlist armies of these creatures? There are certainly enough skeletons in the world for them to do that."

"Don't even think of it," Ember said. "We've got to do something before then. Maybe form militia units to go out and fight these creatures when they're spotted? We'll need to require that they be shifters, Fae, or perhaps even vampires. But then again, what will we do if the vampires prove to be affected by the dragons?"

"That I don't even want to think about. But you're right, we should form a few militia units. We'll have to get permission from the United Coalition, I imagine. Or maybe we can enlist the Fae militia—they're still training in TirNaNog and Navane."

At that moment, Herne gave a triumphant cry and we looked over to where they were standing. All the skeletons were broken to pieces, and the men were pulverizing the bones that were left. I folded my arms across my chest as Ember and I returned to the sidewalk, and then walked across the lawn, not getting too close should any stray bones still be creeping around. But we could see the damage done.

"Are you guys okay?" Ember asked.

Kipa nodded, breathing hard. "Yeah, I've got a few

scratches on me, though. Luckily, I'm most likely immune to any poison they may have had. Do they usually carry poison?"

I shook my head. "No, not usually. Not unless they're carrying daggers, and it looks like these walkers weren't. So what do we do now?"

"You tell us. You know more about skeletal walkers than any of us. Should we clean up the bones?"

"You know, you might want to bring Akron in and have him douse the area with holy water. It would probably end any residual magic that might still be around." I looked around the cemetery. "Do you know how many hundreds of people are probably buried here? We better keep a guard out here, in case the dragon twins decide to come back and build a few more of their toy soldiers."

"That's a good idea," Herne said. "I'll make a few calls." He moved to the side.

I turned to Ember. "Are we still on for tomorrow? To go over to the veterans home?"

She nodded. "Yeah, so get a good night sleep. I have a feeling we're going to be run ragged over the next few weeks. Because you *know* that pair isn't going to stop with just a few skeletal walkers."

"Yeah, I know. That's what scares me."

Kipa and I walked back to my car after saying good-night to the others. I wasn't sure what Herne was going to do about a guard, but that was up to him. Kipa tossed his mallet in back, and I stretched out in the front seat, leaning my head back against the headrest. I fastened my seatbelt, and as he put the car into gear and pulled out of the cemetery, I couldn't help but glance down the road toward the area where the veterans home was. I could see phantoms here and there, wandering the streets, unable to be seen by most others. As we drove past them they looked toward the car, noticing my energy. I just looked back at them, too tired to figure out who they were or why they hadn't crossed over.

"Tomorrow is going be one hell of a day. I'm glad that Sejun gave me something to help me to sleep, because I'll need it."

Kipa nodded, and turned the radio to a classical station. "When we get home, I'll give you a back rub and you can take a long bath and then go to bed. Would you like cookies? I'm not very good at baking, but we can stop somewhere and pick up some."

I laughed. "You're too good to me, and I thank you for that. And no, I don't want cookies, but some ice cream would be fun. I think we're out."

We stopped at a Frosty Freeze and Kipa ran inside, coming back with a bag full of different flavors. "I couldn't decide what sounded best, so I got several I know you love, and a couple I like. Do you think two and a half gallons is too much? I think I got five quarts."

Relaxing, I shook my head and poked my nose in the bag to see what he got. "No, and I'll guarantee you that if we give Raj some, this will be gone by tomorrow. Let's go home and put on an old movie and climb into bed with Raj and ice cream and just chill."

And that's what we did.

CHAPTER THIRTEEN

KIPA HAD BREAKFAST READY BY THE TIME I GOT UP. HE WAS quickly becoming a decent cook, at least for simple things. And the kitchen was clean, unlike when he had first attempted to cook for me.

"Do you have to go into the office today?" I asked.

"Unfortunately, I got a message from Mielikki's Arrow. She wants me over there for a few days. Will you be all right here without me?" He slid a plate of eggs and bacon in front of me, along with the stack of toast points. I loved toast, and two slices were never enough.

I was about to answer when my phone jangled. I glanced at the caller ID.

My mother.

"Hello?" I said, holding the phone to my ear. I wasn't about to put her on speaker. I never knew what she was going to say and even though she seemed to like Kipa, I was still cautious about her interaction with my friends.

"I thought I'd show up tomorrow morning. Will that work for you?" That was my mother. Down to business.

"Sure. It'll be good to see you again," I said. And I meant it. Mostly.

Phasmoria was an intimidating force, and she was about as far from an apple-cheeked, aproned mother holding a plate of cookies as you could get. But she was handy in a fight, and she had my back—that much I knew. For a long time I had resented the fact that she had left me with my father, but now, after some time and reflection, I realized that it had been for the best. I wouldn't have thrived if I'd had to live in the Morrígan's Castle. And life among the Bean Sidhe wasn't a barrel of fun for any child.

"Good. I'm bringing you a present. Will your young man be there?"

I tried not to crack a smile. To hear my mother refer to Kipa as my "young man" was hilarious. But truth be told, if you paired them off in a fight against each other, I wasn't sure which one would survive. Of course, the gods were immortal, but I imagined that Phasmoria could inflict a buttload of damage on Kipa before he managed to disarm her. He was extremely polite to her whenever they met—and I had never seen him be as polite to anybody else.

"He has to head over to Finland for a few days. So it depends on how long you're going to be here."

"That depends on what we're going to be doing. What are you up to?"

I groaned. I hated telling my mother about situations I got myself into because she was always a smartass about it. She'd help me out when she could, but she was a smartass.

"I'm headed over to an old veterans home today to try and corral an ancient creature that has decided to wake up. I happened on it by accident, and at first I thought I woke it up. But then we discovered that it works on a cyclic timeframe. Oh, and the Dragonni have hit Seattle. We took care of some skeletal walkers last night."

My mother was fully aware of Typhon and the damage he was bringing with him. In fact, she had been the one to warn me first that I would be on the front lines, dealing with the collateral damage. For once in my life, I wished she had been wrong.

"Well, isn't that lovely? How are *you* doing? Also, you and I are going to have quite a talk about why you didn't tell me what happened to you until after the fact."

"How could I have told you what was happening to me when I was in the middle of it? Pandora had me tied down to a stone slab, and she was pulling off my nails and teeth. I couldn't very well text you at that moment."

I rolled my eyes, and Kipa stifled a snort. "Parents," he mouthed.

"Yes well, that's true enough. But you should have called me the moment they rescued you. I would have come immediately." The concern was apparent behind her words, even though they came out as criticism.

"Thank you for caring."

"Of course I care. I'm your mother, child. I'm not some stranger. You carry my blood in your veins, and I will always be here for you. Speaking of which, have you told your father about what happened to you?"

I grimaced. "No. It would hurt him too much. I don't want him to know. And don't you tell him either!"

"We'll talk about it when I get there. I'll see you tomorrow." And with that she hung up.

I stared at the phone, shaking my head. "Sometimes

I'm grateful I didn't grow up with her. Honestly, I love Phasmoria, but she is a pain in the ass."

And with that, I got busy eating my breakfast so that I could get over to the agency.

Kipa packed an overnight bag and, after giving me a long kiss good-bye, headed out in his truck. I made sure the wards and security system were set, told Raj to be good and left him snacks, and headed out in my car.

It took me an hour to get across the bridge thanks to rush-hour traffic, but I finally made it over to the agency and parked in the parking garage. I jogged across the street toward the building, glancing up at the overcast sky. It had to be seventy-five and it was muggy as hell. I stopped, staring at the thunderclouds. A flash of lightning streaked across the sky, skipping from cloud to cloud, and thunder rumbled right behind it. The clouds opened and a drenching rain came pouring down, soaking me within seconds. The streeps began to run for cover as I held out my arms, letting the downpour soak me through. The lightning charged me up and even though I was wet, it made me feel alert and ready for action.

As the rain drenched me, I sputtered and jogged up the steps to the building, pushing through the front door just as another round of lightning came through, this time the thunder lagging a few miles behind it.

Deciding it best to forgo the elevator, I headed up the stairs. "Hey." I waved to Angel as I opened the stairwell door and ducked into the waiting room.

She stared at me for a moment, then jumped up. "You

stay right there. I'll get you a towel. You're dripping everywhere."

"Good morning to you *too*," I said, raising my eyebrows. At that moment, Yutani came charging around the end of the hall, stopping short when he almost ran into me.

"I take it it's raining?" He ran his gaze over me, arching one eyebrow.

"Oh, are you a smartass too?" I wrinkled my nose, grimacing. "How much garlic did you eat?" He reeked, like he had just come off of a garlic farm or from an Italian restaurant.

"I know, I know. I took a shower but I couldn't get it all off. It's coming through my pores." He gave me a wry grin, shrugging. "I couldn't help it, I went to an all-you-can-eat buffet and they had the *best* garlic bread there, along with spaghetti and lasagna and—"

"You're making me hungry and I just ate breakfast."

"There are some croissants in the break room, along with half a cheesecake that Angel brought in." He turned abruptly and headed back toward the hall.

Angel reappeared, carrying a large towel. "Here you go, towel yourself off. Viktor and Ember are waiting for you. I'll tell them you're here. If you want some coffee, it's made."

I nodded. "That would be good. At least the storm broke and that should counter some of the mugginess. But it's pouring out there."

"I wouldn't worry about that, or at least I wouldn't worry about it interfering with your plans. Ember and Viktor have worked in the rain before, so get prepared to be soaked even more." Laughing, Angel pointed toward the break room. "Go ahead and go on back. I have work to do or I'd come with you."

Luckily my hair was still braided, and while it was wet, it was manageable. I headed to the break room, laughing gently. My dress was clinging to me like a wet T-shirt, but my denim jacket covered my boobs and that was all that mattered.

Viktor and Ember were waiting. They waved as I entered the room. I tossed the towel over the back of one of the chairs and sat down as Ember jumped up to pour coffee for me. She set the cup in front of me along with the cream and sugar, and then sat back down.

"You still game to go out there? I know it's so wet that a fish would drown out there. And also, lightning." Viktor grinned as another flash illuminated the room.

I counted. One. Two. Three—the rumble of thunder shook the walls. Three miles away, by best estimate. "Well, none of us are going to wear a lightning rod on our heads, I assume? Or any sort of spiked helmet? So yeah, I'm game. A little thunder and lightning can't stop me. In fact, it recharges me. Although things will be a lot more spooky over there. Remember, there's no electricity in the building, so bring flashlights along with whatever else you need."

"I know you've been busy, and so have we, but Yutani did a little more digging into the Lykren. He came up with some more information on how to best attack it." Ember texted me a file, and then pushed a printed page across the table so I could see it. It was a drawing and suddenly it occurred to me I could have looked in my bestiary for information on it. Hindsight was 20/20, though.

"Well, that's certainly an ugly sucker," I said, pulling the page toward me.

The drawing of the Lykren first struck me as some sort of hunched-over ape man/fisherman/frog. Bipedal, the creature had a bowed back, rounding into a froglike head. Its arms were orangutan-like, and its legs were like a man's legs, only with frog flippers for feet. The mouth was filled with serrated edged teeth, and its eyes were beady and narrow. A tongue lolled out from the corner of its mouth, and a pool of drool had been drawn below it.

"Good gods, he's ugly. What's the story with him?"

"Well, nobody's quite sure whether he's reptilian or mammalian, but he certainly looks to be a bit of both. Picture that drawing at about seven feet tall and you have an idea of his size. He's massive, but he can slip through narrow cracks because apparently his bones are malleable."

"*Of course* he is. We have to be so lucky."

"I'm not sure exactly how that works, but he can sneak through a crack five to six inches wide."

"Freakshow contortionist," I said. "What else?"

"The drool that comes out of his mouth? It's poisonous. Or rather, acidic. It can burn your skin in no time flat. And it will burn through leather as well. So you're going to have to be careful—we're *all* going to have to be careful. The acid can cause festering burns, and I have the feeling it will work just dandy on Fae and Ante-Fae skin, and half-ogres."

"What else does it have besides acidic drool? Oh, and the ability to suck out life energy?" This was just getting better and better. A giant frog-ape who drooled acid and fed off of energy.

Viktor snorted. "Did you have to ask? Well, see those fingers? And those really long claws he has for nails? They're serrated, and they can sever flesh as quickly as they can cut butter. So try to stay out of its reach as well."

I tossed the paper back on the table. "All right. Anything else?"

Ember nodded. "Its feet and hands have suckers on them, which means it can actually climb up the wall and onto the ceiling. So the Lykren could drop off of the ceiling in a dark corner and ambush you. Oh, and its tongue? Works like a frog's tongue when it's trying to catch insects. And it's strong. Other than that, I think that's about it."

"Wonderful. And you think we'll find this in the basement of the hospital?"

"From the research that Yutani did, there's probably a hole in the basement that leads down into an underground chamber where it makes its nest during the time it's hibernating. We not only need to kill the Lykren, but we need to destroy the nest just to make sure it didn't lay any eggs. Oh, did I mention that it lays eggs? And that it's hermaphroditic and can reproduce asexually?" As Ember finished, Herne came into the room. He headed toward the coffee pot.

"Hey, how goes it?"

I rubbed my temples, feeling a headache coming on. "Well, we're after a hermaphrodite asexual frog-ape that oozes acid, has serrated claws, feeds off life forces, can crawl up the wall onto the ceiling, and has a power trip going. You want to come with us?" I was only half joking. It would be nice to have a god along.

"I wish I could, but I'm in the middle of looking for the

dragon twins, trying to find out where they're holing up in Seattle. I called Ashera this morning after she talked to you last night and you're right, Aso and Variance have been spotted around town. Now I just have to figure out why they're here and what they want. Besides to cause general havoc."

"I would almost rather face the Dragonni than the Lykren. At least they don't use acid." I laughed, but Herne shook his head.

"Don't be so sure. Some of the dragon folk have acidic spittle. I can't remember quite which ones, or whether they're on our side or Typhon's side, but I do know that at least one type of them has that. And it might be the Reds. Be careful, and be sure to take enough weaponry with you." He stirred sugar and cream into his coffee and carried it, along with a handful of cookies, out of the break room as he headed back to his office.

"All right, I suppose we better get out there. We'll want to go down to the basement, to look for the Lykren's lair. While I saw its reflection, I have a feeling it was just projecting its energy toward me, so it can do that as well. How long do we have before this thing goes back into hibernation? And wouldn't it be safer just to wait until it fell back asleep before we hunted it down?" The idea of the sneak attack was sounding better and better to me.

Viktor shook his head. "Unfortunately, no. When it goes into hibernation, it slips between worlds and the opening to its lair is almost impossible to find. We'd have to wait another seventy years. Granted, all of us will be around then, but we shouldn't put it off. The Lykren seems more active this time than it did the last time. And the last time it was active there were at least ten unexplained disappearances near the veterans home. There's another matter as well. The vortex on which the hospital is built seems to be growing stronger. We aren't sure why, but it's going to be attracting more entities and they may alter the pattern of the Lykren's cycles. In other words, they might be able to shorten it."

I pushed myself back from the table with a loud sigh. "All right, you've got me convinced. We need to take the sucker down. I wish Kipa were here, but he had to go over to Finland this morning."

"We can take care of this. Don't you worry!" Ember sounded more cheery than she had any right to be. But facing a problem with confidence usually made things go a little bit better.

Viktor gathered our weapons—the Lykren was best fought at a distance so Ember was carrying her bow Serafina, and Viktor was carrying a long sword and a spear—and we headed out to Ember's SUV. My magic was at full strength, and I ran through the repertory of spells that I could use.

"By the way, how is this thing against fire?"

"Actually, the Lykren seems extremely susceptible to damage from fire, so your magic is going to come in handy here," Ember said.

Blessing the fact that Yutani had done so much research for us, I rode shotgun with Ember as Viktor climbed into the back seat. We fastened our seatbelts, pulled out of the parking garage, and headed for the veterans home.

I PULLED out my phone and glanced at Ember. "We're going to need more help than we've got. I know you're not fond of him, but I'm calling Trinity. There's a good chance he won't answer. It's not four yet, but it's worth a try." My gut told me we needed him, and I didn't like ignoring that little voice. In the past, when I had, it'd gotten me in trouble before, a whole lot of trouble.

"All right." As she changed lanes, she gave me a sideways glance. "Maybe you're right. Maybe I am underestimating him. I'll try to be nice and I'll try to trust him. He seems to mean a lot to you."

The way she said it made it sound like a question. I knew what she was asking, because she had indicated her suspicions before. "Trinity is nothing more than a friend. But I think he's becoming a good friend, and those are rare and to be cherished when we find them. I'm not going to give up all my male friends just because I'm in a serious relationship—"

"Hold on!" Viktor said. "Serious? So have you and Kipa used the *L-word* yet?"

I blushed, waving to shush him. "Hush. And yes, we have. Both of us. It's official, we're in love. Are you going to give me a box of candy now? Some roses? Maybe you'd like to pay for a nice dinner out for us?" I paused, then remembered that Viktor had troubles of his own in the love department. "How's Sheila doing? How is she healing up? We've all had our share of troubles lately, haven't we?"

Right around the time Pandora kidnapped me, some psycho had sliced Viktor's girlfriend's throat. She had survived, but there had been some question as to whether she would be able to talk again.

"Thanks for asking. She's all right. They haven't caught

the guy, though, and I swear if I ever get near him, he's dead meat. But Sheila has healed up, or rather she's healing up. The stitches are out, and she's able to talk, although her voice is still rough. All in all, it could have been far worse." He paused, then added, "I was on my way to propose to her that night. I haven't yet, because I didn't want her associating my proposal with a bad time. Now I'm not sure what to do. I mean, I still want to propose to her, I want to get married. But I don't want it to seem like an afterthought."

I glanced at Ember and rolled my eyes. "*Men.*" I looked back at him over my shoulder. "Just take her out to a nice dinner and propose. That's all you have to do. Let her take it from there."

Ember was strangely quiet, though I knew why, having talked to Herne.

"All right, all right. I'll make a date with her for Sunday night, and I'll propose to her then. That's Litha, the solstice, so it will be special." He pulled out his phone and was about to text her when I stopped him.

"Don't *text* the woman. Not when you're setting up a proposal dinner. Call her. You said she can talk now."

"She's going to hear the nervousness in my voice."

I snorted, turning back around to face front. "Whatever. It's *your* proposal. Do it your way." I pulled out my own phone and texted Trinity. HEY, CAN YOU MEET US AT THE VETERANS HOME? I FOUND OUT WHAT'S DOWN THERE. WE'RE FACING A NASTY CREATURE. WE COULD USE THE EXTRA HELP. ARE YOU WILLING TO GIVE IT A GO?

To my surprise, he actually texted me back. MEET YOU THERE.

"Trinity will meet us there. Thank you, guys, for giving

him another chance. I don't know what he did to give you such a bad impression." But I did know, thanks to Herne. It wasn't anything Trinity had said or done—it was just Trinity himself. He gave off energy from his soul father, and that was what set them on edge. But I couldn't tell them because Herne had sworn me to secrecy.

"Never let anybody say that I don't give someone a fair shake," Ember said. "Plenty of people don't do that for me, and I know how it makes me feel."

The rest of the way to the veterans home, I stared out the window.

In a way, Ember and Trinity had a lot in common. Both had a family history that came back to bite them in the butt. Ember had loved her parents, but they had still let her down in the end. And Trinity—his mother couldn't forgive him for being a product of the union she hadn't wanted. And his fathers, both physical and soul, had no interest in him. Even though my own upbringing had been a little skewed, the fact was I loved both of my parents. And they loved me. Which reminded me.

"My mother's coming for a visit."

"Do you think she'd like to help us? I'm pretty sure a Bean Sidhe could go up against the Lykren without too many problems." Viktor sounded extremely hopeful.

"Oh for the sake of the gods, no. The last thing I need is her on my back while we're taking down a monster. She's still pissed that I didn't let her know what happened with Pandora."

"Don't feel too bad. My mother still gets on my case when I don't let her know how I'm doing," Viktor said. "I guess once you're a parent, it's hard to let go. Look at

Herne. Morgana and Cernunnos routinely whip his butt, metaphorically speaking."

And with that, we ended the conversation as we pulled into a parking spot near Broadfen. I took a deep breath as I got out of the car. It was time to go monster hunting, and I sure as hell hoped that we'd be the ones with the upper hand.

CHAPTER FOURTEEN

We hadn't even reached the chain-link fence into the garden when I heard a shout behind me. I turned around, wiping the streaming rain out of my face, as Trinity jogged down the street toward us. I waited until he got near before going over to him.

Ember and Viktor glanced over their shoulders, gave a little wave and then continued on toward the fence. As Trinity and I began to follow them, I filled him in on what we were facing. I quickly ran down everything that had happened to me during my initial trip, and then the information we had about the Lykren.

"You say it only comes out of hibernation every seventy years or so?"

I nodded. "Although it lives on the physical plane a good share of the time. But it can project imagery, and it feeds on life essence as well as bodies, we think. If we don't get rid of it now, chances are it will vanish for another seventy years. And who knows what will happen by then? For one thing, it appears that the vortex is growing stronger and attracting more entities. If it grows *too* strong, and the Lykren is still here, maybe it will strengthen the creature as well. Whatever the case, we don't want to take any chances."

Trinity nodded. "And there are just the three of you? Are you sure that's enough to fight it?"

"Unfortunately, we're all we have right now. Crap! I was going to ask my neighbors—Meadow and Trefoil—to help, but I forgot and it's a little late for that at this moment."

"All right. I'm in. What can kill it?"

"It can be damaged by physical attacks, but the problem is getting in close enough to hit it. Not only does it siphon off life energy, but its acidic drool and serrated claws aren't helpful either. It has a lot of defense mechanisms, and remember the clown face that I saw? Apparently, the Lykren can project some of your worst fears."

"You're afraid of clowns?" Trinity smirked.

We were approaching the chain-link fence where Viktor and Ember were waiting.

"Don't judge. Clowns are evil and scary." I thought back to the Harlequin, back when I was a kid. I had tried to hide that memory, burying it deep, but after I brought it up the other day, it was now at the surface of my thoughts. Maybe that was a good thing, though. Maybe that would keep the Lykren from digging it out of my subconscious, although I had plenty of other fears it could work off of.

Trinity gave Viktor and Ember a two-fingered salute. "So I hear we're going monster hunting?"

"That's about the size of it," Viktor said he examined the chain-link fence. "Do we just crawl over this?"

I nodded. "There's no gate right here. And the only gate that I found is on the inside, leading to the central hospital building."

Viktor stepped over the chain-link easily. Placing one hand onto the railing, Ember grasped the bar with her other hand and swung herself over. I climbed my makeshift steps and Viktor surprised me by reaching up and taking me by the waist, then swinging me down. I flashed him a warm smile and he smiled back. Trinity easily jumped the fence, and I led them through the knee-deep vegetation, swishing it around me as it tickled my legs. One of the dried blades of grass caught my finger and cut deep, and I yelped. The sting was like a paper cut and it set me even more on edge.

As we reached the gate leading into the courtyard, I pointed to the two residence halls on either side of the secret garden.

"Those, I gather, were convalescence residences. There are ghosts everywhere around here. I see them and feel them all over the grounds. My guess is that the spirits are being trapped here by the vortex. I'd like to see them move on, but I don't know if it would do any good. A vortex that big—with that many ley lines going through it —well, it's just going to keep sucking them in." I paused at the gate, my hand on the lock. I really didn't want to go back in there. "I'm creeped out as hell about going back in."

"We're here," Ember said. "It will be all right."

I opened the gate, heading in. This time, with Trinity with us, I wouldn't have to pick the lock. I turned to him.

"Last time I was here I picked the lock, and then I

locked it up when I left. Can you unlock it? Or it's going to take us a while to get in there."

Trinity nodded, heading forward toward the door. We hurried to catch up with him. As he got there, he placed his hand on the knob and I heard him whispering an incantation under his breath. I couldn't catch the words, but a moment later there was a click and the door unlocked.

"That is a handy skill to have," I said.

He shrugged. "It does come in handy, but it earns me a bad reputation as well. Not that I give a fuck." He paused, glancing over his shoulder at us. "Who wants to go in first? I don't think I'm going to volunteer."

Viktor moved to the front. "I will. Here, let me through. Ember, why don't you bring up the rear just in case anything tries to ambush us. Weapons out, people. Although Raven, I imagine you're going to be gathering your magic instead?"

I nodded. "I think you'd rather have me working magic than trying to wield a blade. I can hit a target accurately, but poison won't stop a ghost."

Trinity opened the door just a crack. "Here, go ahead and push it all the way open. If I let go of the knob while it's still closed, it will just lock again. The moment it swings shut behind us, it will lock. Which means you better hope that I survive this so I can get you guys out here."

I snorted. "I could pick the lock, but we don't want me fumbling with that if there's something after us."

Viktor pushed the door open, and it squeaked. I grimaced, wishing I had brought an oil can with me. Viktor headed in, his flashlight casting a wide beam, and

Trinity followed him. I came third, and Ember swung in behind me. The moment we were inside and the door shut behind us, I shuddered. The place really did give me the creeps, and not just because I knew about the Lykren. It was just so filled with lost souls and trapped spirits that it left me totally unsettled and melancholy.

Viktor glanced around, swinging his flashlight from side to side. "I assume you checked behind the counter?"

"Yeah. There wasn't much there. I was upstairs on…" Good grief, I couldn't remember which floor I had been on when I saw the clown in the window. "I don't know what floor it was. But I was upstairs when I saw the Lykren's image."

"Okay, but we need to head down to the basement to find its lair. My guess is that it just projects itself from there." Ember paused. "*Crap.* Yutani was going to try to get the blueprints, but I forgot to ask about it. All right, we do this the hard way. Where would the basement be?" She began flashing her light on the doors. Some of the signs were still attached.

We passed the exam rooms, and then the staircase leading up. Once we reached the end of the corridor, we turned to the left.

The spirits of the veterans suffering from various PTSD flocked through the halls, crowding in along with the ghosts of some of the people they had killed in battle, all wound together in a tangle of karmic connections. I watched their expressions—they all looked adrift and lost.

Trinity broke away from us, skirting ahead along the inner wall as he examined the doors. I wanted to call him back, but I realized that he wouldn't listen to me. I could see

Viktor tensing up ahead of me and I heard him mumble something under his breath. A moment later Trinity turned around, pointing to the door that he was standing in front of.

"Basement," he said in a soft voice that carried down the hall toward us. I realized that he had modulated it, focusing it so that only we would hear it. Or at least, I *hoped* only we would hear it. We hurried over to him, and as we approached, he tried the knob, jiggling it. He paused, looking up as the door cracked just the faintest distance.

"Unlocked," he said. He let go of the knob and stood back, returning to his place in line in back of Viktor. Viktor glanced over his shoulder, giving Trinity a grumpy look.

"Please don't break off on your own unless we're in combat. You could get us all killed, either by us trying to find you, or by you leading something back to us. Whatever the case, talk to us before you decide to meander off on your own."

Trinity stared up at him, eyeing the half-ogre with an unreadable look. But all he said was, "Sure thing. This is your rodeo."

I hoped he meant it. Trinity was unpredictable and chaotic as hell, and now I knew why, but I couldn't very well explain the reason to the others, especially in front of him.

Without another word, Viktor turned back to the door and opened it, shining his light down the steps. They were concrete and steep, and they bent to the left at the end of the staircase.

With a deep breath, Viktor glanced back. "Ready?"

We were, and so he turned back to the stairs and we began to descend.

THE BASEMENT WAS GLOOMY, given there were no windows to the outer world and the only lights we had were our flashlights. Their beams offered scant comfort, and somehow the shadows cast as we descended the stairs seemed more threatening than the darkness itself. A little voice inside urged me to cast a fire spell, to set some piece of wood blazing as a torch, but I knew that would be a faint comfort, no real protection, and it would use up my spell energy.

Viktor reached the landing and held up his hand, motioning for the rest of us to wait where we were. He peeked around the corner to check out what we were getting ourselves into. Seconds later, he popped his head back and looked up the stairs at the rest of us.

"Another stairwell going down, with a sign that says the basement is down there. But there's a door to the side of the landing, leading to what looks like an underground level of the complex. I didn't know there were any extra floors down here, except the basement."

"Me either," I said. "Where should we look?"

"I think the Lykren would have its lair in the basement," Ember said. "If it's coming up from underground, it had to burrow in somewhere and that's the most likely place. Viktor, is the door locked?"

He disappeared for a moment, then reappeared. "No, it's unlocked. I had a quick peek inside and it looks like there are a lot of records there. Metal shelving with stacks of boxes on them, and filing cabinets lining at least one of the walls. You'd think they would have taken the records with them, or destroyed them."

"Maybe they were shut down so abruptly that they didn't have time. I imagine the government would have wanted to keep the records for evidence, but then again— if the files are still here, either they were returned or never confiscated. Whatever the case, I vote that we head toward the basement proper," Ember said.

Viktor motioned for us to follow him. "I think you're right. Let's go."

We followed him around the bend in the stairs, and I glanced at the door on the landing as we passed by. It was impossible to tell where all the ominous energy was emanating from. It seemed to surround the entire complex. It seeped into everything—every wall, every door, every square inch seemed rife with a feeling of doom.

There was a metal door at the bottom of the basement. Ember, Trinity, and I waited a few stairs up in case Viktor had to turn and run when he opened it. He cautiously held up his flashlight, giving us a questioning look.

"While I'd love to be able to turn it off and catch whoever is in there unawares, no way in hell should we go in blind. We'd be sitting ducks." I shook my head. "Keep that light on."

Ember and Trinity murmured their agreement, so Viktor prepared to open the door. He held the light directly in front of him, in hopes of startling anybody who might be on the opposite side. We had to take any advantage we could get.

The Lykren was susceptible to fire damage, so I

summoned up fire into my fingers, focusing on the element rising within me. I didn't want to cast the spell too soon or it might fizzle out, but if I cast it too late, the Lykren would have a chance to attack. Magic was a tricky business, and required a steady hand and even steadier nerves.

After a moment, Viktor put his hand on the knob, and started to tug open the door.

It was locked.

"Damn it," Viktor said, glancing back over his shoulder at Trinity. "Can you open this?"

Trinity headed down the stairs, motioning for Viktor to move out of the way. As the half-ogre shifted places, Trinity put his hand on the doorknob and whispered his incantation again. There was a soft click as the door unlocked. He turned the handle, motioning for Viktor to take over. Viktor grabbed the knob before it could lock again, and—as Trinity backed up—Viktor quickly opened the door and shone the light directly in front of him.

I squinted trying to see what was in there, but all I could see was a large cavernous room, filled with furniture and bric-a-brac. There were trunks and boxes that looked so old that their hinges had rusted shut, and spiderwebs and cobwebs draped from shelf to trunk to box, cloaking the room like a veil of tattered lace. I shivered. Even though I wasn't all that afraid of spiders, the thought of walking through the sticky webs gave me the creeps.

With a deep breath, Viktor headed in, pulling out his sword to cut away the cobwebs. I followed behind Trinity, and Ember behind me. As the door shut behind Ember, we heard it click again. Great, we were locked in.

I was trying to gauge our surroundings, to make sense of where we were, but there was so much junk that it was hard to tell. I couldn't see most of the walls; there were bureaus and rusty metal cabinets and stacks of boxes everywhere, cluttering the room. Shivering, I moved over to Trinity's side and was surprised to see that Ember had followed me.

"I guess we just start skirting the room. Keep your eyes open for any tunnels breaking through the walls, or even up from the floor. We don't know where the Lykren broke in from." Viktor let out a sigh, looking frustrated.

"Is something wrong?" I asked, although I suspected I already knew the answer.

"No, but I just had a thought. What if its lair is in another building? What if it made a tunnel over here? I just feel like we're working with a jigsaw puzzle," Viktor said.

"There's no help for that," Ember said. "So keep looking. And shout if anything happens. Viktor, you examine the south wall, Raven, you take the east wall, Trinity— why don't you check the north wall, and I'll start here." She divided the room into quadrants.

As much as I dreaded poking around on my own, I dove into my task. I headed into the labyrinth of castaway goods. There were trunks everywhere and, as I flashed my light on them, I saw that they each had names stenciled on the top. I realized they came from the soldiers, probably the ones who died here. Why they had never been returned to the families, I didn't know, but maybe they too had been confiscated for evidence and just forgotten about afterward.

I finally reached the wall and began to trace the length

of it. I scanned from floor to ceiling with my flashlight, but by the time I was nearly at the end I had yet to find anything.

Hand on my hip, I stared at the inner part of the room, which was piled high with debris. The junk pile would be the perfect place to build a lair, I thought. It would be hard to get into, and not visible right off the bat. But then again, the Lykren had had no reason to think anyone would be coming after it. Still, it couldn't hurt to take a look.

As I headed toward the biggest pile of junk, Ember let out a scream from the west wall. I froze, unable to move as a wave of energy rippled through the room. Suddenly, everything seemed to loom over me and I cowered, terrified of the dark, terrified of the unknown. I wrapped my arms over my head, whimpering.

A little voice inside whispered, "It's the Lykren," and I tried to push through the fear, but I couldn't. I was paralyzed. I tried to call out, but once again Ember shrieked, and at that moment I broke free, my mind telling me to run, to get out of the basement. I found myself running toward the stairwell door. As I raced past Trinity, he reached out and grabbed hold of me, pulling me close. He wrapped his arms around me as I struggled, and his voice, soft and persuasive, cut through the haze of fear.

"Hush, girl. It's just the fear spell. Take a deep breath and let it out slowly, make sure your wards are up." His voice was so sensuous that it overrode the cloud of terror.

All I wanted to do was follow his orders. I did as he asked, forcing myself to stop fighting his hold. I began to breathe deeply, and I was in the middle of clearing my chakras when I realized he had charmed me. That alone was disconcerting, but right now it had been the best thing he could do. I took a slow, deep breath, holding it for a few seconds before I let it go. My fear went with it.

Viktor let out a shout. "It's got Ember! Hurry!"

"You okay?" Trinity asked.

I nodded, and we raced over to where Viktor stood, just in time to see Ember being dragged into a tunnel. The creature that had hold of her was massive. There was no mistaking it—it was the Lykren, all right.

"If I cast a fire spell, I'll hit Ember as well. You're going to have to fight it."

Viktor and Trinity swung into the tunnel, which was well over eight feet tall. I followed behind them, pulling Venom out from her sheath. Hopefully, the Lykren would be vulnerable to poison.

Up ahead, the tunnel spread wider into a shallow cavern, and we could see the Lykren clearly in the glow of several torches that had been placed in sconces along the tunnel walls. It looked as hideous as the drawing that we had seen. The creature had hold of Ember and she was struggling in its grasp. One of its massive arms was wrapped around her waist as it half-carried, half-dragged her along.

Trinity pulled out a pair of throwing daggers, and before Viktor or I could say anything, he aimed and tossed. The daggers spun through the air, whirling around and around to plunge into the Lykren's shoulder. It let out a scream, dropping Ember as it reached back to pull out the blades. Ember scrambled up and away, racing toward us as fast as she could. The Lykren let out a grunt and it was then that I saw a long fissure in the rock wall next to it.

The fissure was small, barely six inches across, but the Lykren began to morph, squishing together as though it were made of Jell-O. Before we could do anything, it vanished into the crack in the wall and we were standing there alone.

CHAPTER FIFTEEN

WE STARED AT THE CRACK THAT THE LYKREN HAD MANAGED to squeeze through. There was no way in hell any of us could even begin to try and fit ourselves in there.

Ember shook her head. "We need to come back when we're better equipped. I wasn't expecting this."

Relieved to hear her speak, I backed away toward the entrance to the tunnel.

"Are you okay?" I flashed my light over her, and let out a gasp. There was blood pooling around her ankle, saturating her jeans. "What happened to your leg?"

Looking confused, Ember looked down at her leg and gasped. "I'm bleeding! I don't know how that happened!"

I knelt by her side, wincing as I peeled the leg of her jeans up, while Trinity held the flashlight for me. There was a long gash in her ankle and it was bleeding profusely.

"We have to bind this up and get you back to the office. You need medical attention," I said. I turned to Trinity. "Do you have a spare rag or something?"

He nodded and without a word, he pulled out a clean handkerchief and gave it to me. I was starting to wrap it around her ankle when Viktor shouted, "Look out!"

The next moment, something grabbed hold of me and tossed me across the room. I landed face-first, skidding along the floor. Dazed, I rolled up, looking back to where I had been kneeling. The Lykren had emerged from the crack, and once again, it had grabbed hold of Ember's arm, trying to drag her away again. Viktor had hold of her other arm and Trinity had wrapped his arms around her waist. The Lykren was trying to squeeze back through the wall, trying to take Ember with him.

Holy fuck, it was going to try to squeeze her through that crack. And with its strength, it might succeed in doing so, although it would kill her in the process.

I dragged myself to my feet, using one of the metal shelving units to brace myself on. I had to stop him, and that meant bringing up fire. That also meant I might catch the rest of them in the process, but Ember was swearing up a blue streak.

"Let go of me, you mother pus bucket!" She was screaming, and I could tell it wasn't just anger giving voice to her fury. The Lykren had managed to drag her arm, up to the elbow, into the crack but her elbow proper wouldn't fit. And that wasn't a deterrent to the monster, as it kept tugging on her. Ember screamed again, this time in pain.

I close my eyes. There was only one spell that would work without engulfing Ember and the others. I seldom used it because it was so powerful that it would drain me dry, but it had a focalized target area, and I would be less likely to hurt the others.

"Everybody, close your eyes!" I shouted. Then, I began the invocation.

> *Fire of heaven, I call thee down,*
> *from top of cloud to kiss the ground.*
> *Bolts to forks, forks to bolts,*
> *I summoned thee, a million volts.*
> *Strike to true, I set the mark,*
> *jump from heaven, to Lykren arc!*

There was a deep rumble overhead, shaking the building with its force. A dark cloud appeared near the ceiling, swirling in a mass of mist and smoke. I focused on the crack, focused on the vision of the Lykren, focused on the force that was building as I held out my hands toward the fissure. And then, praying that the spell would work right, I called forth the lightning. I drew it down from the heavens through the cloud that had formed, then into my body and sent it out my fingertips.

The force of it shook me to the core, rattling my teeth in my head, sending every hair attached to my skin into full attention. The lightning bolt ripped out of my hands, aiming toward the crack over Ember's head. With a hop, skip, and a jump, it leapt from my hand to hit the wall, piercing the crack at least three feet above Ember's head.

Thank the gods, it missed Viktor and Trinity as it slammed into the granite, widening the crack, sending a shower of stones and sparks every which way as it exploded. The lightning bolt funneled into the fissure and we heard a loud screech, and then Ember tumbled back, falling on the floor as she knocked into Viktor and Trinity, taking them with her.

Panting, I started to brace myself against the metal shelf unit, and received a spark so powerful that it set me flying across the room again. I landed near the others. Feeling singed in every part of my body, I sat up, with a ringing in my ears so loud I couldn't hear anything else. Panting, I turned and crawled over to where Ember lay. There was a nasty wound on her arm, and at first I thought that my lightning had done it. But when I looked, I could see the festering. No, that looked like an acid burn. The Lykren must have drooled on her. Her arm also looked bent in an unnatural way.

Viktor and Trinity were shaking their heads, and they were staring at both Ember and me, confused looks on their faces.

"We have to get out of here," I said, not knowing whether I was shouting or whispering because I could only hear the ringing in my ears. "I'm not sure that thing's dead. I don't want it coming back for us."

I had exhausted my magical resources for the day, that was for certain. Viktor jumped up, scooping Ember up in his arms. I thought I could hear her scream but I couldn't tell. Trinity grabbed up a flashlight and leading the way, he headed back toward the door. He yanked it open, holding it for Viktor. I followed, unsteady on my feet, and Trinity closed it behind us. He muttered something under his breath and I realized he was locking the door.

We stumbled up the staircase, and while I could see spirits all around, they kept their distance, eyeing us warily as we passed by.

When we reached the ground floor, Trinity led us directly to the nearest exit, and again, using his abilities, unlocked the door and opened it so we could slip out. We forced our way through the foliage back to the secret garden.

I wanted no part in touching anything metal at the moment, and Trinity seem to realize that because he opened the gate for us. I was still dizzy, but I managed to stumble along after Viktor and Ember. Trinity caught up to me and slid his arm around my waist and I put my arm around his shoulder. He helped steady me, keeping me on my feet as we headed back to the chain-link fence.

Once there, Viktor easily stepped over, Ember still in his arms.

But I just stared at the fence. I wanted no part in touching it because I still felt electrified. Trinity said nothing, but scooped me up in his arms and lifted me over to the side, setting me down before he jumped over himself. As we hurried along Broadfen, the rain continued to pour down, washing away some of the soot that had clung to me from the lightning bolt. It also flattened my hair, which was sticking out in all directions. But my focus was on Ember, who had fallen unconscious.

We made it back to the car, where Trinity opened the doors, helping Viktor load Ember in the back seat. Viktor fished her keys out of her pocket and swung around to the driver's side. Trinity bundled me into the passenger seat, and then he crawled in to sit beside Ember. I glanced over my shoulder and saw that he was once again trying to bind up her ankle. Viktor started the car and we headed back to the agency, far worse for the wear than we had left it.

Viktor pulled up directly in front of the office. We lucked out and found a parking spot directly by the building. I turned to him.

"Thank gods there's an urgent care clinic on the first floor of your building," I said, glancing back at Trinity and Ember. "How is she?"

Trinity shook his head. "She's breathing, but still unconscious. And she's bled quite a bit. That wound on her arm also looks bad, and her arm might be broken. We need to get her inside as soon as we can. She may need more help than the urgent care clinic can give her, so call Herne down in case he has to go call Ferosyn."

He helped Viktor ease Ember out of the back seat. She was still unconscious, so Viktor swept her up in his arms and began to jog up the steps. Trinity darted around him, to open the door. I followed a little more slowly, feeling like every nerve in my body had been toasted. I had a looming headache, and even my teeth hurt.

As we entered the building, I pulled out my phone and tried to call Herne, but it wouldn't work. I stared at it. It wouldn't even turn on. I had fried it when I threw the lightning bolt. I veered off from the guys, heading toward the stairwell.

"I'll go get Herne. My phone is dead." I tackled the stairs, which normally wouldn't be a problem. Four flights of stairs? Nothing to it. Except when I had let a lightning bolt use me as a catapult. I managed to reach the landing of the stairwell on the fourth floor and opened the door. Angel was sitting behind her desk and she glanced up as I staggered in. The look on her face was priceless, and I would have laughed if the circumstances were different. Instead, I suddenly felt like my knees were going to give out. I stumbled forward a couple steps and then collapsed, the room spinning.

Angel jumped up, calling for Herne. He poked his head out from his office, took one look at me, and rushed over to my side. Angel took my other side and together, they lifted me to my feet. Herne caught me up and carried me back into the break room, sitting me on the sofa near the window. He went down on one knee beside me. "Where the others? What happened? Ember, is Ember okay?"

Rattled and weary, I leaned my head back. "Herne, you need to get down to the urgent care. Ember's there. She's been hurt. I'll be okay, I'm just dizzy and wiped out."

Angel sniffed my hair. "You smell like ozone."

"No shit, Sherlock. I just ran a million-volt lightning bolt through my body. Every inch of me tingles in a not-so-nice manner." I wanted Kipa, wishing he were here instead of in Finland.

Herne leapt up, heading for the door. He turned around, glancing at me. "You should come down too, to make certain you're all right. Here," he said, hurrying back to my side.

He once again picked me up and, ignoring my protests that I could walk, he silently carried me out to the elevator. Angel followed him, pushing the button as we waited in the waiting room. I struggled briefly, but Herne just gave me a squeeze and I stopped. At that moment Talia and Yutani came out from their office, took one look at me, and rushed over. Talia started to say something, but Angel held up her hand.

"You go with Herne and Raven down to urgent care. I'll watch over the office here. But let me know what's going on," she said, giving Talia a stern look.

Talia nodded. As the elevator opened, Herne stepped inside, followed by Talia and Yutani. Talia pressed the first floor button, and I leaned my head against Herne's shoulder, another wave of dizziness sweeping through me. Talia glanced at Herne, a question in her eyes.

"Apparently she ran a massive lightning bolt through her body," he said. "I didn't even know you could cast a spell like that," he added, looking back at me.

My mouth felt fuzzy and dry, but I finally found my tongue. "I rarely try it. It's hard, and it totally drains me of energy, but we had no choice."

I groaned again, feeling queasy, and closed my eyes as I rested my head back on his shoulder. He didn't say a word, just held me firmly in his arms, and when we arrived at the first floor, he carried me over to the urgent care clinic. Yutani opened the door and Herne swept in to the reception room.

I was in and out by that point, feeling scrambled beyond measure, and I could hear Herne saying something to the receptionist, but I couldn't quite make out what it was. I must have blacked out for a bit because when I woke up, I was laying on one of the exam tables, propped up, with a blanket over me. A doctor was taking my pulse.

"I'm one of the Ante-Fae," I whispered, my throat drier than ever. "Our physiology is different than even that of the Fae."

She gave me a nod. "What is your pulse supposed to be?"

"Sixty-five at rest. Eighty if I'm stressed."

She frowned. "It's ninety-five. Herne said that you cast a lightning bolt?"

I nodded. "Yeah. It's not the same thing as being struck by lightning, but it leaves a residue."

"Well, you smell like smoke. I think you'll be all right, you just need a day or so to heal up. I suggest you let them take you home and put you to bed and let you sleep it off."

"I need a shower. How's Ember?" I glanced around, noticing Herne was nowhere to be seen. However, Yutani was sitting in a chair nearby, leaning back as he waited.

"She'll live. She's beat up, though. She had a dislocated shoulder, a festering wound from what looks like some sort of battery acid, and Dr. Bonner is sewing up her ankle. She'll need at least forty stitches. Something gave her one hell of a gash."

I nodded, knowing exactly what had happened to her. "She's lucky that's all that happened," I said, "considering what we were up against."

I started to sit up but a wave of dizziness washed over me and I slammed back against the raised bed, groaning. "My phone. My mother's supposed to be coming for a visit and now she won't be able to contact me. What the hell am I going to do?"

My mother would be livid when she couldn't reach me, and once she found out why, I'd be in for far worse. I glanced over at Yutani. "Can you get my phone working again? Please?" I suddenly realized I wasn't wearing my regular clothing, but a hospital gown instead.

Yutani held up my phone. "I've got it here," he said. "I'll see what I can do with it. If you're okay, I'll head back to the office and see if I can get it back into commission."

I nodded. "I'm not going to be dancing on tables any time soon, but I'll be okay." As he left the room, I turned back toward the doctor. "The truth about Ember? Will she survive?"

"She'll survive, but she's out of commission for at least a week or two. And you should be, too," the doctor said, glaring at me, shaking her finger. "You hear me?"

I let out another groan. "I can't make any promises, but I'll try."

BY THE TIME I got home, I could barely make it out of the car without shaking. Trinity had driven me; he wouldn't let me touch the wheel. While it was covered with leather, I was still getting sparks every time I touched anything metal.

We eased into my driveway, and I froze. There were lights on in the house, and I hadn't turned them on when I left in the morning. I glanced at my watch. It was barely 4 P.M., and the rain had just started to ease. Trinity jumped out of the car and ran around to the side, opening my door. He helped me out of the car.

"The lights—I didn't leave them on," I said, pointing as I began to shake, panicking. Raj was in there. Suppose somebody was in there hurting him? Ignoring the pain, I stumbled forward, but Trinity caught hold of me and helped me up the driveway.

"I'll unlock the door," he said, reaching for the knob, but it opened right before he could touch it. Kipa was standing there.

He took one look at me and grabbed me up. "Sweetie, are you all right?"

I pounded my fists against his chest. "You scared the

hell out of me! What are you doing home? I thought you were in Finland?"

"Herne texted me that you were in the urgent care clinic. He told me that you were hurt and so of course I came home. Mielikki understood." He took a long look at me, then shook his head. Turning to Trinity, he asked, "What the hell happened to her? I can feel how jarred she is. And her hair looks…" He paused.

I reached up and smoothed down the locks but despite the rain, my hair was still one massive mane of frizz. And I still had patches of soot on me, along with nerves that were so raw I could barely stand to be touched.

"She'll be all right. I just wanted to make sure she got home all right," Trinity said, then he gave me a quick wave. "I'll call later to see how you are." Before I could say a word, he turned and headed off.

Kipa carried me into the living room as I started to tell him what had happened.

"I decided to run a million-volt lightning bolt through my body just for fun," I said, the words drifting away. There, in the rocking chair, was my mother.

Phasmoria stood slowly, looking like a hard-core dominatrix. She was wearing black leather pants, a silver mesh tank top, and a black leather jacket. Her hair hung loose, down to her waist, with one brilliant silver streak through the jet-black strands. She was wearing stilettos, and her lips were as black as her outfit. Her eyes were cool, with barely any color at all in them. They were as frosty as snow, as frosty as the grave.

Phasmoria strode forward, gathering me out of Kipa's arms. She carried me over to the sofa and glanced over at Kipa. "Blanket, please. A sheet would be good. She's not going to want to mess up her sofa with all of that soot."

Kipa jumped to obey. He brought a blanket and spread it out, and Phasmoria slowly eased me onto it. She sat beside me, taking my hand. We weren't a family of huggers, we were barely demonstrative with each other, but we really did care.

"What is this about you running a lightning bolt through you?" she asked.

"I had to. We're fighting a freaking weird-assed monster and the only thing I could do to prevent it from dragging off my friend Ember was to shoot a lightning bolt at it."

"Did you hit it?" Kipa asked.

I shrugged. "I don't know. The thing squeezed into a crack that was barely six inches wide. We couldn't follow. It tried to take Ember with it and dislocated her shoulder. It also drooled on her so she's got a nasty wound on her arm, and it sliced up her leg. She's sporting forty stitches. I sent the bolt into the crack and blew up a shower of stones from every which direction, so I know how deep the bolt hit. But whether it hit the Lykren or not, I can't say for sure. "

Kipa stood. "I'll get you some tea if you like, and a sandwich?"

I shook my head. "Dude, sometimes food isn't the answer. Neither is tea. But I'll take a glass of sparkling water, with lots of ice." I leaned back on the sofa, trying to relax.

My mother took my hand. "Do you think Typhon had anything to do with this?"

I shook my head. "With the Lykren? No, but we're

seeing signs of him in so many places. Two of the Dragonni are in Seattle, causing problems. They animated a
group of skeletal walkers the other night that we had to
put down. But we don't know where they are right now."

As I sat there, Kipa pulled off my boots for me. He
tossed them to the side and began to rub my feet. I let out
a little moan. Every muscle in my body hurt.

"Do you have any Epsom salts? Or Dead Sea salts? "
Phasmoria asked.

I nodded. "I actually do have some Dead Sea salts.
They're in my ritual room. Why?"

"They make an excellent relaxant. Kipa, why don't you
go draw my daughter a bath? Lukewarm. And add a
handful of the salts. If you can't find them, I'll come help.
Make sure the water isn't too hot—she's had too much
heat running through her body as it is."

"Yes, ma'am." Kipa scrambled up, hurrying off toward
my bedroom.

Phasmoria watched him go, waiting till he vanished
out of sight. Then she turned to me. "I have a present for
you. Remember, I said I was bringing one?"

I frowned, wondering what it could be. Knowing my
mother, it could be just about anything. "What is it?"

"Just wait and see. I'll be right back." She sounded
really excited and I hoped that, whatever it was, I could
muster up some enthusiasm. Right now, all I wanted to do
was sleep.

I stretched out, closing my eyes while she was off in
the guest room. A few moments later, she returned,
carrying a long, narrow box. She motioned for me to sit
up before handing it to me.

The box was wrapped in a giant red ribbon with the

bow on top. I stared at the box, wondering what the hell she could have in there. Given my mother was Queen of the Bean Sidhe, it could be just about anything. As I untied the bow and slid off the ribbon, I held my breath. Lifting the lid, I peeked inside.

There, lying on a cushion of velvet, was a beautiful wand made of yew. I gasped and pulled it out of the box, holding it up so that I could examine it. The wand was gorgeous, with carnelian and citrine, sapphire and amber inlaid on the wood. At the top was a tiny amethyst sphere, about an inch in diameter, set in a bronze setting. Copper wire wound around the wand down to the handle, which was wrapped with a strip of bear fur. As I wrapped my hand around the wood and set the box on the floor, everything felt right. Even through my frazzled nerves, it felt like a perfect fit. The wand felt like an extension of me.

I looked up at my mother. "Where did you get this? It's beautiful."

Phasmoria laughed. "Let's just say someone owed me a couple very big favors. I asked them to make that for you. It just felt like time to give you something—a tool that is made for you and only you. Since you aren't following in either my footsteps or your father's footsteps, we had to combine ideas into the best one we could come up with. The wand is from both of us. I hope you like it." Her eyes gleamed and for once, her voice felt warm and tender.

I set the wand down on the coffee table and repositioned myself, sitting up so I could lean my head against her shoulder. She wrapped her arm around my shoulders, and I closed my eyes, breathing softly. I hadn't snuggled with my mother for years.

"Thank you, Mother. This is incredible. I didn't expect anything like this."

"Mother always knows what her daughter needs," Phasmoria said. And with that, she gave me a kiss on the forehead, and the next thing I knew I was stretching out on the sofa with my head on her lap. Sometimes it was nice to have your mother at home. Sometimes, family made all the difference.

CHAPTER SIXTEEN

When I woke up the next morning, I expected to feel every aching bruise in my body, but I was surprisingly pain-free. I wasn't sure whether it was the herbal concoction that Sejun had given me or it was the bath or the blend of tea that my mother had made for me before bed. Whatever the case, I woke refreshed, able to get up and head for the shower without even a single wince.

Kipa was already up. Fretting that he was probably talking to my mother, I padded into the bathroom and this time, I was able to take my time and lather up with my favorite bath scent. The night before I had taken a half-hour long bath and I had still felt jarred by the electricity that I had funneled through my body. This morning, I was able to wash my hair and fully get rid of the smell of soot and smoke.

As I dried off, and did my hair and makeup, I texted Ember to see how she was doing.

How are you feeling this morning? Yesterday was a clusterfuck.

She texted back within minutes. I'M AT HOME. ANGEL AND HERNE WOULDN'T LET ME COME INTO WORK TODAY. I'M ON CRUTCHES FOR A FEW DAYS UNTIL MY ANKLE HEALS, AND MY ARM STILL ACHES LIKE HELL FROM BEING DISLOCATED. ESSENTIALLY, I'M ROLLING AROUND THE BOTTOM FLOOR OF THE HOUSE IN A WHEELED DESK CHAIR. MR. RUMBLEBUTT LIKES TO RIDE ON MY LAP. HOW ARE YOU? I'VE NEVER SEEN A JOLT OF LIGHTNING LIKE THAT. I CAN'T IMAGINE HOW IT FELT TO HAVE IT COMING THROUGH YOU.

I frowned, deciding it was taking too long to text, and called her instead. She answered on the first ring.

"I wondered if it wouldn't just be easier to call," she said. "So where the hell did that spell come from? I didn't know you could do that!"

"I wasn't sure I could. Technically, I knew the spell. I've known it for a while now. But when push comes to shove, the fact is I've never cast it before in my life. I wasn't sure exactly what would happen, except it was the only choice I had to avoid engulfing both Viktor and Trinity with my fire as well. And you, of course. I knew that I could direct the lightning bolt to a target well above your head. Do you think it hit the Lykren?"

Her voice was soft when she answered. "I don't think so. I think it startled him, and maybe you injured him, but my gut tells me he's still down there. We'll have to go back in after him, I'm afraid."

I snorted. "*You* aren't going anywhere in your condition. You get to sit this one out, and be glad you do. I'm about to head down to breakfast. My mother showed up last night, and Kipa was here, too. Herne texted him to get his ass back from Finland. Thank heavens Mielikki didn't mind."

"Well, you don't think you're going back in there either, do you?" Ember sounded almost offended when I told her she couldn't go.

"Not without a hell of a lot of backup. Herne said to call him when I got up, so I guess maybe he's going to help after all. And with Kipa here, well, I trust the pair of them to help us put the creature down. I had no clue the Lykren would prove *that* dangerous. How's your arm feeling? That wound looked horrible."

"It feels like somebody decided to dribble acid all over me, that's how it feels. But I'm on some sort of painkiller they gave me. It's safe for the Fae to take, and it mutes the pain, but it makes me a little loopy. But I don't ever want to see anything like that creature again."

"I wouldn't knock wood on that, if I were you. Chances are both you and I are going to face far worse in the coming months, if not years. I imagine Herne is trying to find the dragon twins?" It hadn't escaped my memory that we were facing a far greater enemy than the Lykren.

"I think he is. He won't talk to me about it right now, though. He just keeps saying don't worry and get well. You know, I love him, but sometimes it drives me nuts when he tries to protect me. Just because I can't go out and fight right now doesn't mean I don't want to know what's going on."

That was one thing I liked about Ember. She wasn't afraid to look reality in the eye, and usually she'd spit at it afterward. "I'd better go. I'll try to find out whatever I can about the dragons and I'll let you know, if Herne won't tell you. Is Angel with you today?"

"No, she's at the office. It's just me and Mr. Rumblebutt. And quite honestly, I can use some downtime. But don't you tell anybody!" Laughing, she hung up.

I finished dressing and then headed downstairs to start the day.

MY MOTHER and Kipa were nowhere to be seen. Raj was sitting at the table, in a chair, trying to eat pancakes off of a plate. I stared at him, shaking my head. Raj never ate at the table. He said it made him uncomfortable.

"What is Raj doing?" I asked, walking behind him and leaning down to give him a hug.

"Phasmoria decided Raj should eat at the table like civilized people. Raj does *not* want to make Phasmoria mad, so Raj let her fix him blueberry pancakes and put him in a chair. Can Raj eat on the floor, now that she's outside?" He sounded so plaintive that I laughed, picked up his plate, and set it in the corner where he usually ate. He scrambled awkwardly off the chair, lumbering over to his dish.

"So my mother's outside with Kipa?" I asked, eyeing the stack of untouched blueberry pancakes on the counter.

"Yes. Kipa and Phasmoria are arguing about what to plant where. Raj wanted no part of the argument, so Raj just focused on his blueberry pancakes."

"Raj is a very smart gargoyle." I stabbed three of the pancakes, placing them on a plate and drowning them in maple syrup. I added a couple of hard-cooked eggs along with a stack of bacon. As I filled my plate and then made a triple-shot cappuccino, I headed back over to the table and sat down on the side where I could see Raj. I wasn't in any hurry to go break up an argument over gardening.

I had almost finished my breakfast when the door to the backyard opened and Kipa came in, Phasmoria right behind him. The two were still embroiled in an argument, apparently. I listened to them for a moment, trying to figure out what they were butting heads over, and realized it was still something about the herb garden. I ignored them, polishing off my food before wiping my mouth and turning to them.

"If you two are just going to argue every time you're together, maybe I'll have to find something for you to really argue about." I stood, picking up my dishes and heading to the kitchen.

My mother was dressed in a pair of blue jeans, a Metallica T-shirt, and a leather jacket. She looked like a classy biker chick. Kipa, on the other hand, was wearing a pair of cargo shorts and a sleeveless hoodie. I glanced outside. The sun had returned, and even inside of my house, the mugginess had dissipated. The storm had broken it.

"Just because he's a god doesn't mean that he knows his herbs. I *have* to know my herbs, because I supervise the gardeners for the Morrígan. And I will tell you right now, you've got them planted all wrong. We're going to have to dig up the entire garden and rearrange everything. You get much better results that way."

I tried not to roll my eyes. My mother was convinced she knew just about everything. The annoying fact was, she was usually right. Shrugging, I said, "Fine. If you want to dig up my garden and rearrange it, feel free. Kipa can help you if he likes. I'm not that interested in getting my hands in the dirt, not unless it's graveyard dirt."

Kipa snorted. "Have you talked to Ember this morning?"

I nodded. "After I took my shower, yes. She's doing better, but she's not going to be running around anytime soon. She's at home right now with Mr. Rumblebutt."

Raj perked up, swinging around to stare at me. "Raven take Raj to visit Mr. Rumblebutt? Raj likes Mr. Rumblebutt."

I groaned. Raj might like Mr. Rumblebutt, but Mr. Rumblebutt did *not* like Raj. The cat vanished under the bed every time I took Raj with me to visit Ember. For a fifteen-pound Norwegian Forest cat, Mr. Rumblebutt could move.

"Maybe we'll just wait on that for a while. After all, Grandma Phasmoria is here. Raj wouldn't want to ignore her, would he?"

My mother stared at me, then chuckled. "I'm grand-mother to a gargoyle. Oh well, I can think of a lot worse grandchildren to have. And Raj knows that I love him."

That was one thing I could say for my mother. She was an animal lover, and she extended that love to Raj. Even though he was more of a Crypto than an animal, she treated him just like she would any other talkative puppy dog.

Suddenly remembering that I hadn't taken care of the ferrets yet, I jumped up. "I need to tend to the ferrets—" I started to say, but Kipa stopped me.

"I took care of them this morning while you slept in. I just got a text from Herne. He wonders if you and I will come down there to the office today to talk about the Lykren."

I nodded. "Yeah. We still have to deal with it." I turned to my mother, a cajoling smile on my face. "Hey, you want in on this?"

Phasmoria leaned back in her chair, brushing back her hair from her face. She pointed to my cappuccino. "If you make me one of those, yes, I'll go with you."

"Sounds good. I'm going to go change in case we head out from the Wild Hunt to take care of the Lykren. I don't think I want to waste a pretty dress on that creature. And yesterday's clothing smells like soot."

As I headed back to my bedroom to change, Kipa called out, "You aren't going to fight!"

"Make my mother her cappuccino!" I smiled as I shut the bedroom door behind me. It felt good to see them getting along. The arguments were a cover, I knew that much, and right now, two of the three most important people in my life were here with Raj and me. I just wished my father would come visit, but he had postponed his trip till autumn.

As I stripped out of my clothes and found another old minidress that could go over shorts and leggings, it occurred to me that we made for a mighty strange little family unit. An Ante-Fae, her Lord of the Wolves lover, her Queen of the Bean Sidhe mother, and her pet gargoyle. Yes, we were truly the perfect little nuclear family.

HERNE WAS WAITING for us at the Wild Hunt, along with

Viktor, Yutani, and Talia. Angel was at the desk but couldn't leave because she was on a call, so she waved for us to go on back. As we entered the break room, Viktor glanced up, a worried look on his face.

"How are you doing today?" he asked me. "I swear, I'm surprised you even survived. How that lightning bolt passed through you without crisping you from the inside out eludes me."

I shrugged. "I guess that's the way my magic works. It didn't leave me unfazed, I'll tell you that. Everyone, I'd like you to meet my mother. I'm not sure if you've met Yutani or Talia or Viktor before, although I think you've met Herne."

Herne gave Phasmoria a short bow. The others waved at her, Talia looking a little unsettled.

"So you've come to help us?" Herne asked.

Phasmoria flipped a chair around to straddle it, leaning her elbows on the back. "If you think I'm letting my daughter go in there without backup, you can forget it. And I don't think I can stop her from coming along, so I'm not even going to try." She gave me an indulgent look, and I felt she was actually proud of me.

"Well, I can say I'm glad you're going to be there," Viktor said. "I'm not looking forward to another battle with that creature. I think we need to plan out how we're going to take it down before we go in. At least now we know what we're dealing with."

"The Lykren can squeeze through passages six inches wide, if not smaller. And it will try to take you along with it. That's what happened to Ember. So it has incredible strength, and if it gets hold of your arm or leg, you can pretty much bet you're going to have at least some nasty cuts—if not a detached limb. Those serrated claws are sharp. I'm surprised Ember still has her foot attached." I shook my head. "Also, acid. Remember—the acidic drool."

"Well, she was wearing heavy leather boots, and I'm sure that helped, but both her boots and her jacket are in rags from both the claws and the acid." Herne held up a leather jacket that I recognized as belonging to Ember. The left arm was slashed in multiple places, and there was a blistering gap on the forearm where the drool had landed.

"Yeah, that's the damage it can do." I shook my head.

"How do we kill it?" Yutani asked.

"I believe that I actually hit it with my lightning bolt, but I don't think it died. It might have taken some damage, though, so it could be wounded if we're lucky." I frowned, tapping my fingers on the table. "Unfortunately, I'm still drained from casting that spell. I don't have much to go in with except possibly a few flame strikes, but I can't do that if anybody else is close to it. The lightning bolt was much easier to aim at a single target. Flames can spark out to catch everybody else in their wake."

"Never you mind that," Phasmoria said. "You'd be surprised at what I can do. And that wand I gave you? I hope you brought it."

I nodded, reaching in my tote bag to pull it out. As I set it on the table, Herne gasped.

"Is that what I *think* it is?" Herne asked, leaning over the table to look at it. He glanced up at me, then over at Phasmoria. "Where did you get this?"

"Never you mind," Phasmoria said. "It was a gift to me —consider it payment for a debt. Now, I'm giving it to my daughter."

I eyed the interaction between the two, wondering what the hell was going on. "So what does the wand do? Last night we didn't talk much about that."

"Last night you weren't fit to talk much about *anything*. The wand is actually an artifact of sorts. So you'll want to be very careful with it and hold onto it. I'm sure there are others who wouldn't mind stealing it from you." My mother took an imperative tone. In other words, *pay attention to what I'm saying.*

"Um, just *who* owned it and what is it?" I was starting to get a little nervous. Artifacts were rare, and they were prized by treasure hunters. The fact that my mother had told me she got it from someone who owed her a favor made me nervous. Phasmoria's ethics were similar to my own, but she stretched them a little more than I did.

"I paid a little visit to Baba Yaga. She owed me a great deal of money for the last poker game we played. She was eager to settle her debt. This is the wand of Straha, the Fire Witch of the Black Forest."

I gasped. My mother had told me the story of Straha when I was young, but I hadn't realized that she actually had anything to do with her. "You've *got* to be kidding!"

"Who's Straha?" Yutani asked.

Phasmoria looked across the table at him. "I'll tell you the abbreviated story and at some point Raven can fill you in on the full tale. Straha, the Fire Witch of the Black Forest, was an extremely arrogant sorceress. She had come to her power through a deal with a demon, given she had no innate magical abilities of her own. It was said that she sold him ten children from the village for her powers."

"Oh, this is starting out just lovely," Talia said.

"Yes, well, it gets better. The villagers were so terrified of Straha that they didn't bother pressing over the loss of their young ones. Thanks to the demon, Straha had power over fire and death. She worked very strong death magic, and she was a malicious and vicious old woman. But she still wasn't happy." Phasmoria snorted. "You can't please everybody."

"What was she upset about?" Herne asked.

"Straha thought that the deal with the demon included a return of her youth. It did not. The demon told her if she wanted her youth back, she'd have to pay him every cent in the world she had, and Straha was rich. But another attribute of Straha was that she was a parsimonious old biddy. So she kept her age."

Talia shook her head. "How long did she live after that?"

"Long enough that she was able to fashion several wands and charge them with her own essence. The magic sustained her, so she didn't die like most humans. She lived for several hundred years after that. This was the first wand she made, and it carries the power of fire and lightning within it. It can only be used once before it must be charged up again—and it has to be charged under the new moon. But the damage it can do is monumental. Raven could level an entire house with one use of the wand. I trust it will help during the altercation with the Lykren."

I stared at the wand, unable to formulate a coherent sentence. The fact that my mother had just given me the power of a small bomb that I could use once a month blew my mind.

I looked up at her. "You really *do* trust me, don't you?"

Phasmoria laughed then, leaning back in her chair. "Oh my daughter, I trust you to use it wisely. You're growing in your power, and I don't know if you have any idea just what you're evolving into."

I wanted to ask her what she meant by that, but before I could, everyone else burst out talking about the wand. I stared at it as it sat on the table, in the center, hoping that I truly did have the wisdom to use it.

WE WERE ready to head out. Herne volunteered to drive. Viktor and Yutani were going, along with Kipa, Phasmoria, and me. Yutani had brought the whip that his father had given him, and Viktor had borrowed Ember's crossbow, Serafina. Herne had several powerful weapons of his own, and my mother... Well, my mother had her own powers.

I sat in the second seat, the wand on my lap. My mother sat on one side, telling me how to use the wand and I was trying to focus on what she said, but all I could think about was what was waiting for us. Also, if I ended up using the wand, would there be anything left of the building?

"What are you thinking of, love?" Kipa was sitting on my other side.

I shook my head. "I don't know, to be honest. The wand. The Lykren. The fact that we're going to be chasing down dragons soon enough. I guess... Too many thoughts to put into words."

He leaned down, and—giving my mother a quick glance—pressed his lips against mine. When we came up for air, he whispered to me, "I'm here. I'll be here for you as long as you need me. Try not to get rattled. We have a long ways to go before the journey's over."

Wondering what he meant by that, I was about to ask when we pulled up to the curb, parking near Broadfen. As soon as my mother was out the door, I followed her. A million thoughts were whirling through my head, and I just wished I could get focused, because I knew I was going to need it.

CHAPTER SEVENTEEN

GOING INTO BATTLE THIS TIME FELT FAR LESS DAUNTING. With two gods and my mother joining us, I wasn't nearly as frightened. I still wasn't looking forward to the ordeal, but the fact was that now we were more than evenly matched. All we had to do was summon the Lykren out from hiding again. We discussed the matter on the way down the side street, heading toward the chain-link fence.

"If we all go barging in there at once, chances are he won't come out. Maybe Yutani, Viktor, and I should go in while the three of you hide outside the door waiting. That way it will think we're easy pickings. I'll have my wand just in case," I said.

"That's actually a good idea," Herne said.

Kipa scowled for a moment, but murmured an agreement. I could tell he didn't like it, but he wasn't going to stop me. We wanted to get this over and done with as soon as possible and I didn't want to have to come back here again.

We came to the chain-link fence and before I could

start climbing over the top, Kipa swept me up and sat me down on the other side, then leapt over the fence himself. He turned to offer my mother his hand, but she'd already skimmed the top and was standing beside me. Herne, Viktor, and Yutani joined us.

"Which building?" Herne asked, glancing around at the surrounding facilities.

I pointed to the hospital building. "That one there." Somehow the building didn't seem so threatening this time, most likely due to the company I was in. I had to admit, having friends in high places—the divine sphere, that was—made a difference in my courage.

I clutched my wand, trying to remember exactly how my mother had told me to use it. There was an amber gem in the center of it. If I touched that gem with my thumb and incanted the spell, it would trigger the wand. I had to make sure I was pointing it in the proper direction, though, because the resulting blast could level walls. And I had to pay attention where I was holding it. Luckily, the amber gem wasn't in easy access while I was carrying it by the end, but it still would pay for me to be clearheaded and paying attention at all times.

Without Trinity, it took a little longer to get into the building. Kipa was able to pick the locks, though, and soon we were inside. I gave Herne directions to find the basement, and with him in the lead and my mother behind him, we headed toward the stairwell. Kipa was bringing up the rear to keep guard on us.

I noticed that the spirits were taking much more attention of what was happening. They were focused on us, staring with their mouths open. It had to be the divine energy, I thought. Plus, with my mother's nature, the spirits would totally be onto us. Several of them actually took one look at her and sped off in the other direction. I couldn't help but grin, thinking that I had my own Mommy Dearest, only Phasmoria could beat out Joan Crawford any day.

We reached the basement door, and I stared at the metal. There were dents in it, as though something had tried to punch through from the inside. I remembered that Trinity had locked the Lykren in, and apparently the Lykren didn't have a key. I pointed to the bulges on the metal.

"I think the Lykren did that. Trinity locked it in with his magic, so it hasn't been able to get out to feed. I'm pretty sure most of the spirits have avoided the basement, relieved at not having the damn thing chasing them."

Herne arched his eyebrows as Kipa went to work on the lock. I wondered if he'd be able to break it, given Trinity's magic, but after a few moments we heard a click and Kipa stood up, brushing his hands on his pants. He tucked away his lock picks and then gave the rest of us a long look.

"I guess this is it," I said. "Viktor, Yutani, and I will go in. Do not let that door lock behind us. And be ready to come in the minute we give a shout."

"Why can't you just use the wand to level the basement?" Viktor asked.

"Because then we wouldn't know if we killed it. Just like I don't know if my lightning bolt did any damage. We have to see the body to make sure it's gone." I bit my lip, not wanting to go back in that room. Even though I had Viktor and Yutani and wasn't going in alone, it still felt about the same thing when it came to the Lykren. The creature was crafty, fast, and deadly.

"Okay, but the *minute* you see it you let us know." Kipa turned me to him, holding me by the shoulders. "I am not taking a chance on losing you."

"Trust me, I'm not interested in offering myself up as a sacrifice. I'm not that selfless." I reached up and kissed him on the nose, then stroked the hair back away from his face. "I love you. Remember that. And thank you for helping me through the past weeks." With that, before he could say another word, I turned to the door and, motioning to Viktor and Yutani, opened it and slid through.

ONCE AGAIN THE room was dark as pitch.

I turned on a flashlight and waved it around, trying to let the Lykren know we were here. This time we weren't going for secrecy. We wanted to attract its attention. We headed toward the tunnel on the west wall, and I hoped that Kipa would remember the directions I had given him.

As we entered the tunnel, I thought I could hear something from up ahead. I waved the light harder, practically playing disco ball.

"Do you think we'll find it?" I asked, keeping my voice loud.

Viktor picked up on what I was doing. "I don't know, but I sure hope not. It doesn't help that there are just the three of us down here."

Yutani stifled a snicker. I glared at him, but he just shrugged. "I doubt if it speaks English, he said. "But that sure sounds like the fakest conversation I've heard in ages."

"That's because it is!" I said, realizing he was right. The Lykren probably didn't understand a word of English. Which was on my side, I supposed.

We came to the back of the tunnel, where we paused for a moment. I peeked into the cavern, trying to find the crack through which it had oozed the day before. There it was, on the far wall. The crack had taken some damage from my lightning bolt—that much was apparent.

I motioned for the men to slowly follow me in. As I tried to close my eyes and send out my sensors, the energy hit me with full force. We weren't alone in the room. The Lykren was here. Now we just had to keep it from escaping until the others could get here.

"It's around," I said. "I can feel it."

"I can too," Yutani said. "It's old, whatever it is, and it's old and nasty."

At that moment, there was a noise to the side and the Lykren came darting out from behind a tall column. It was close enough to brush me with its claws and I screamed, jumping back. It barreled my way, and I tilted the wand toward it, but if I let go now, it would seal us in. Yutani and Viktor were shouting for the others, as Viktor pulled out his sword and slashed at the Lykren as it went by.

He managed to hit it, and the creature turned toward him with an angry hiss, reaching out with those long arms and serrated claws. Its frog mouth opened and its tongue lolled out, heading directly toward Viktor like a weapon.

Holy crap, we hadn't seen that before!

"Jump," I yelled, hoping Viktor could move fast enough.

But Viktor was too slow, and he stumbled over a rock as the Lykren's tongue caught hold of his arm and wrapped around it. Viktor let out a shout, and we heard a sizzle as the acidic drool began to burn through Viktor's leather jacket.

Yutani pulled out his whip, and I realized this was the first time he had had a chance to use it in battle. He hauled back and sent it cracking through the air, to slice across the Lykren's back.

The Lykren let out a shriek, muffled by the fact that its tongue was still around Viktor's arm, and it tried to turn to see what had hit it. There were glistening drops running down its back. I wasn't sure if it was blood or some other sort of liquid, but Yutani had scored a direct hit on it. I could smell charred flesh and it occurred to me that it might be from the ilithiniam. The whip had a magical metal braided into it. From what I understood, the great Coyote had braided the whip himself for his son.

The Lykren was still holding onto Viktor, and I could tell now that its acidic drool had eaten through the leather sleeve, and was biting into Viktor's arm. The half-ogre was struggling, but the Lykren was stronger than even Viktor.

Yutani took another swing, this time aiming for the Lykren's tongue. Instinctively, I winced as the whip came whistling down across the long pinkish organ, slicing right through it. Drool splattered everywhere, sizzling as it hit the floor and as it hit Viktor and Yutani. Luckily, I was far enough back to escape it, but both men screamed as the acid burned into their skin.

At that moment Herne, Kipa, and Phasmoria burst through the tunnel. I darted out of the way, yelling, "Viktor's hurt, and I think Yutani has been too."

They took in the situation, and Herne immediately pulled out his bow. He nocked an arrow and let it fly. The arrow pierced the Lykren in the forehead and bit deep. The Lykren shrieked and stumbled back.

Kipa took that moment to swing in behind it, plunging his sword through its back. The Lykren shrieked again and began to waver. Phasmoria moved in at that point, and she held out her hands toward it. A gray smoke began to filter through the air, emanating from the Lykren's eyes and mouth as she sucked it in, drinking deep.

I had never seen my mother in action before, and while her kind usually foretold death, they could easily mete it out as well. She drank deep, her laughter shaking the room as she suddenly spun into the air, half corporeal, half mist. She threw her arms wide as her head dropped back and the last of the Lykren's life vanished down her throat. Her eyes were glowing, and she gave a long look at us before settling back down and regrouping into herself.

The Lykren was slumped on the floor, and Herne prodded it with the sword. It didn't move.

"I think it's dead," he said.

"This place needs to be torn down," Phasmoria said. She shook her head. "The Lykren is only the first of the monstrosities that will come through this area. I'll gather the spirits and take them away from here, but the area itself is a magnet for spiritual activity. The buildings have also been acting like traps. If they are gone, it may help some in the years to come. I don't know if that makes any sense to you, but it does on an energetic level."

"Well, you said this wand can bring down the house. Do you think it can bring down this complex? We can create a local earthquake, so to speak." I stared at the wand, wondering just how powerful it could be.

"I don't know if it can bring down all three, but definitely we should destroy this one. This is the heart of the complex. And this entire complex has almost become a sentient being, given all the energy that's run through it. Go outside. I will gather the spirits and take them out. Then, I'll return and you can give it a try."

My mother shooed us out. As we waited in the secret garden, she returned to the complex. I could hear a great whispering and then a host of spirits rose out of the building, following my mother who was a dark figure in a black cloak flying through the air.

"What are you looking at?" Kipa asked, shading his eyes as he looked up at the sky.

"Can't you guys see her? And all the spirits?"

The others shook their head. None of them could see my mother, and none of them could see the parade of spirits following her.

We sat in the center of the garden for twenty minutes until my mother suddenly returned, stepping out from behind a nearby tree.

"They're gone. I've released them and now they can move on. Okay, my daughter. Give the wand a try like I told you." My mother looked as excited as a kid on Christmas morning.

I snorted, standing up. I moved to the front, where I had a clear aim at the hospital, and held out the wand. Glancing over my shoulder, I looked at my mother.

"This isn't going to hit anybody out in the front street, is it? I don't want to hurt anybody."

She shook her head. "I checked. There's nobody around there. This is a pretty dead area, so to speak. In many ways."

I fastened my hands around the wand, holding the amber gem. Closing my eyes, I focused on the building itself. The building that I had come to hate.

> *Fire, fire, burning higher,*
> *here my will, obey me still.*

There was rumbling, and then the building began to shake. Bricks crumbled as the walls caved in. As we watched, the building slowly imploded, crashing into a pile of dust and rubble. It hadn't spread out to the residences, but at least the hospital itself looked to be fully destroyed.

We stood there for a moment. I stared at the wand, trying to comprehend that I had just managed to destroy an entire building with one little incantation.

Then, before the sirens could draw near, we turned and hightailed it out of the garden, heading back to the office. The Lykren was gone, the spirits were free, and a blot on Seattle's history had been wiped out.

CHAPTER EIGHTEEN

WE WERE HOME BY TWO, JUST IN TIME FOR ME TO GET ready for my appointment with Sejun. I wasn't sure how I felt about sitting down for a therapy session so soon after a major battle, but I ran upstairs to change. At least the blast from the wand hadn't left me feeling like I was electrocuted. I jumped in the shower, scrubbed down, and then quickly changed into a cute purple tiered skirt and a green corset top.

My hair was driving me batty—I needed a trim—so I pulled it back into a high ponytail, and put on huge hoop earrings. As I slipped on a pair of striped tights, Kipa came in the room. I turned, and the moment my tights were all the way up, I raced over to him and threw myself in his arms. He caught me up, whirling me around and then pulling me to him for a long kiss.

"Thank you, thank you for coming back. Thank you for telling me I mean so much to you that you would return from Finland just for me." I wrapped my legs around his waist, letting out a little sigh. If I had my way, I would have stripped him naked right there and yanked him into bed. But a glance at the clock told me that we really didn't have time, even for a quickie. After another long kiss, I unwrapped my legs, and swung down. He grinned at me, his eyes warm and sensuous.

"I'm thinking what you're thinking, I'll give you ten bucks on that. What say we send your mother to a movie tonight?" He winked at me.

"Yeah, I'd like that, except I don't think she actually goes to movies. I don't know, maybe she does. We'll find a way. Here, would you hook this for me?" I held out a long chain. The necklace was one Kipa had given me a few weeks before, a smoky quartz crystal set in a silver pendant. It was almost sixty carats, huge and sparkling.

He fastened it around my neck and kissed me under the ear. "You are brighter and more sparkling than all the gems in the world. How are you feeling now?"

"I'm excited, actually. Destroying the Lykren actually made me feel better. It took away some of my fear, I think. And I think Sejun is going to do the same. I decided that it's fine if he siphons my pain and fear away off of me. I can do without it, as long as he doesn't take my memories with it." I paused. "I hope you don't mind about my friendship with Trinity. Herne told me about his background, and I assume you know about it already?"

Kipa nodded, his eyes darkening. "I will never tell you who to be friends with, and I won't interfere with your friendships. We've had a rather lackadaisical relationship up till now. You've made it clear that you don't want to be one of a group of women I date. And I've honored that.

And now, I actually feel compelled to tell you the same thing. I don't just want to be one of your paramours. I never thought I would find myself opting for exclusivity again. But Raven, as long as we're together, I don't want anybody else in bed with us. Can you promise me that?"

"Of course. When I told you I didn't want to be just one of the notches on your belt, I thought it was implied that I would return the same. Why does Trinity bother you so much? Is it his parentage?"

Kipa led me over to the bed, sitting me down. He crossed his legs after slipping off his sandals. "There's something that connects you and Trinity. I can feel it when you're together. I'm not saying it's romantic. But you two have some sort of a bond. Maybe it's joint interests, maybe it's an understanding because both of you had to grow up too soon. Whatever the case, when the two of you are together it feels like there's nobody else in the room. It's like you close yourselves into a private little world. And I don't particularly enjoy being left out of your world."

"I didn't realize I was doing that," I said. "Trinity and I just seemed to connect. But I am telling you the truth when I say that I'm not romantically interested in him. He's sexy, I'm not going to ignore that. Or deny it. But he's not the kind of sexy for me. I guess the thing is I feel that he understands a part of me that nobody else seems to. Given my lineage, there's a lot of chaos in my life. And sometimes I like to play hard. I'm not sure if you are interested in that. I love clubbing, and dancing, and sometimes I like to walk on the edge."

The somber look on Kipa's face vanished and he leaned back and laughed. But it didn't feel mean or sarcastic to me. "You want to walk on the edge? Oh sweetheart, I can take you to the edge. Trust me. I just didn't know if *you* could accept that part of me. I have a darker side, I'll be honest. Herne is more upstanding, but I run with the wolves and I creep under the moon. I know what it's like to reach out and touch the aurora borealis, to bathe in the energy of the northern lights. I know what it's like to drink away a week while you're out in the snow, dancing around a bonfire. I can drum with the best of them, and if you let me, I'll drum for you, if you'll dance for me."

I stared at him, holding my breath as his words spiraled around me. There was a wildness to them that transcended even the side of me that loved to let go and let loose. No wonder he got along with my mother. They were both feral, two cats in a colony, prowling through the woods at night.

"Maybe I have underestimated you. I've never seen this side of you, and it stirs my blood."

He jumped up. "Come with me, Raven. When I go back to Finland, come with me for a few weeks. I'll show you my homeland, and my forests. I'll introduce you to the witch women there and they can teach you what it means to worship the northern lights. Mielikki won't mind if you come, though I'll ask first. In fact, I think you would really like her. And I think she'd really like you." He was grinning now, looking positively delighted.

"I'd love that. We'll have to wait until my mother leaves, but yes, I'd be happy to go with you. Do you mind if we take Raj? I don't want to leave him alone too long."

"Where we go, he goes. We're all part of the same family—we're forming a tribe, you know." He glanced at the clock. "You'd better get downstairs. Your therapist will be here any minute."

As I headed for the door, I looked over my shoulder. "I'm not giving up Trinity as a friend, but that's all he is. I promise you on my word of honor."

As Kipa pulled out his tablet and started to read, he blew me a kiss and waved me on.

AFTER MY SESSION WITH SEJUN, my mother and I went out for a walk. I told her about Trinity, and about what Kipa had said to me in the bedroom.

"Relationships are complex, aren't they?" she said.

I nodded. "What brought you and Curikan together?"

Phasmoria paused, staring up at the growing dusk. "His kindness. And I love dogs, and his eyes." She frowned, staring at the trailhead leading into the park. "If I could have stayed with him, I would have. I would have stayed and been your mother, and watched you grow up. But I don't think you and I would have as good of a relationship if that had been the case. I wasn't born to be a mother. I was born to be a *queen*. And when you're born to be a queen, duty always comes before family. But I tried my best to be there for you when I could, and I swore I would never just vanish without a word. I'd like to think I've kept that promise."

I settled myself on the fence bordering the park. "You may not have been the best mother, but you've been a good role model. Father took care of me well enough for the both of you. He has so much love in his heart that I think he needs somebody with him now. I wish he would find someone new. I know you two are still friends, but he needs a woman he can dote on. Somebody he can nurture. I've actually thought of asking him to move out here, though I doubt if he would. He's coming for a visit later this summer, though, so I'll get to see him then."

"Your father is a homebody. When he and I both realized that it wasn't going to work out for the two of us, I almost didn't tell him I was pregnant. I was going to have you and raise you by myself to be another daughter of the Morrígan. But when I talked to my lady, she told me *No*. That being her servant wasn't your path. She told me you would grow up a bone witch, and that you had a strong destiny set out before you. And then she told me that I had to let you go. The Morrígan said that I could spend a few years with you, but then I would have to leave you with Curikan and return to my duties. I almost quit that night." She looked up at me, her eyes luminous in the growing twilight.

"What made you decide to obey?"

"I belong to the Morrígan, for one thing. And I had a long talk with someone I hold in high regard. And she told me that sometimes what seems a sorrow will actually turn out to be a joy. She's a bit of a fortune-teller, and I trust her advice. So I did as the Morrígan bade me. I told Curikan I could stay with him for a few years, and then I would have to leave. And I did my best to be a good mother while I was there, and I did my best to explain why I had to leave. I hope you understood, although I never expected that you would."

"I think I did," I said. "As much as I've missed you over the years and wished you were there, I realized that you wouldn't be happy. And if you weren't happy, we wouldn't be happy. Not to be rude, but you can be a handful when you're upset. I also realized that sometimes one parent can make up for both. And you—you're my mother. But you're more of a friend. I respect you and sometimes you scare the hell out of me, but when it comes down to it… I think I'm more like you than I am like Father. And I would never tell him that because I love him too much."

Phasmoria laughed then, and wrapped her arm around my shoulders as we headed into the park. For the first time weeks I didn't feel the park closing in on me and Pandora seemed so far away that I could barely picture her.

My mother and I talked for another hour, walking through the growing twilight, listening to the birdsong. At home my love waited for me with my beloved Raj. I had friends, and even if we were facing a gloom and doom future, complete with dragons and skeletal walkers and all the darkness that felt like it was pouring in, I realized there were still lights in this world. And my friends and family were some of the brightest.

I would never be lost in the darkness as long as they were with me.

IF YOU ENJOYED this book and haven't read the first eleven books of **The Wild Hunt** Series, check out: **The Silver Stag, Oak & Thorns, Iron Bones, A Shadow of Crows, The Hallowed Hunt, The Silver Mist, Witching Hour, Witching Bones, A Sacred Magic, The Eternal Return,** and **Sun Broken.** Book 13—**Autumn's Bane**—is available for preorder now. There will be more to come after that.

Return with me to **Whisper Hollow,** where spirits walk among the living, and the lake never gives up her dead. I've re-released **Autumn Thorns** and **Shadow Silence,** as well as a new—the third—Whisper Hollow Book, **The Phantom Queen!** Come join the darkly seductive world of Kerris Fellwater, a spirit shaman in the small lakeside community of Whisper Hollow.

I invite you to visit Fury's world. Bound to Hecate, Fury is a minor goddess, taking care of the Abominations who come off the World Tree. Books 1-5 are available now in the **Fury Unbound Series: Fury Rising, Fury's Magic, Fury Awakened, Fury Calling,** and **Fury's Mantle.**

If you prefer a lighter-hearted paranormal romance, meet the wild and magical residents of Bedlam in my **Bewitching Bedlam Series.** Fun-loving witch Maddy Gallowglass, her smoking-hot vampire lover Aegis, and their crazed cjinn Bubba (part djinn, all cat) rock it out in Bedlam, a magical town on a mystical island. **Bewitching Bedlam, Maudlin's Mayhem, Siren's Song, Witches Wild, Casting Curses, Demon's Delight, Bedlam Calling, Blood Music, Blood Vengeance, Tiger Tails,** and Bubba's origin story—**The Wish Factor**—are available.

For a dark, gritty, steamy series, try my world of **The Indigo Court,** where the long winter has come, and the Vampiric Fae are on the rise. The series is complete with **Night Myst, Night Veil, Night Seeker, Night Vision, Night's End,** and **Night Shivers.**

If you like cozies with teeth, try my **Chintz 'n China paranormal mysteries.** The series is complete with: **Ghost of a Chance, Legend of the Jade Dragon, Murder**

Under a Mystic Moon, A Harvest of Bones, One Hex of a Wedding, and a wrap-up novella: **Holiday Spirits.**

For all of my work, both published and upcoming releases, see the Biography at the end of this book, or check out my website at **Galenorn.com** and be sure and sign up for my **newsletter** to receive news about all my new releases.

CAST OF CHARACTERS

Raven & the Ante-Fae:

The Ante-Fae are creatures predating the Fae. They are the wellspring from which all Fae descended, unique beings who rule their own realms. All Ante-Fae are dangerous, but some are more deadly than others.

- **Apollo:** The Golden Boy. Vixen's boytoy. Weaver of Wings. Dancer.
- **Arachana:** The Spider Queen. She has almost transformed into one of the Luo'henkah.
- **Blackthorn, the King of Thorns:** Ruler of the blackthorn trees and all thorn-bearing plants. Cunning and wily, he feeds on pain and desire.
- **Curikan, the Black Dog of Hanging Hills:** Raven's father, one of the infamous Black Dogs. The first time someone meets him, they find good fortune. If they should ever see him again, they meet tragedy.

- **Phasmoria:** Queen of the Bean Sidhe. Raven's mother.
- **Raven, the Daughter of Bones:** (also: Raven BoneTalker) A bone witch, Raven is young, as far as the Ante-Fae go, and she works with the dead. She's also a fortune-teller, and a necromancer.
- **Straff:** Blackthorn's son, who suffers from a wasting disease requiring him to feed off others' life energies and blood.
- **Trinity:** The Keeper of Keys. The Lord of Persuasion. One of the Ante-Fae, and part incubus. Mysterious and unknown agent of chaos. His mother was Deeantha, the Rainbow Runner, and his soul father was Maximus, a minor lord of the incubi.
- **Vixen:** The Mistress/Master of Mayhem. Gender-fluid Ante-Fae who owns the Burlesque A Go-Go nightclub.
- **The Vulture Sisters:** Triplet sisters, predatory.

Raven's Friends:

- **Elise, Gordon, and Templeton:** Raven's ferret-bound spirit friends she rescued years ago and now protects until she can find out the secret to breaking the curse on them.
- **Gunnar:** One of Kipa's SuVahta Elitvartijat—elite guards.
- **Jordan Roberts:** Tiger shifter. Llewellyn's husband. Owns *A Taste of Latte* coffee shop.

- **Llewellyn Roberts:** One of the magic-born, owns the *Sun & Moon Apothecary*.
- **Moira Ness:** Human. One of Raven's regular clients for readings.
- **Neil Johansson:** One of the magic-born. A priest of Thor.
- **Raj:** Gargoyle companion of Raven. Wing-clipped, he's been with Raven for a number of years.
- **Wager Chance:** Half-Dark Fae, half-human PI. Owns a PI firm found in the Catacombs. Has connections with the vampires.
- **Wendy Fierce-Womyn:** An Amazon who works at Ginty's Waystation Bar & Grill.

The Wild Hunt & Family:

- **Angel Jackson:** Ember's best friend, a human empath, Angel is the newest member of the Wild Hunt. A whiz in both the office and the kitchen, and loyal to the core, Angel is an integral part of Ember's life, and a vital member of the team.
- **Charlie Darren:** A vampire who was turned at 19. Math major, baker, and all-around gofer.
- **Ember Kearney:** Caught between the world of Light and Dark Fae, and pledged to Morgana, goddess of the Fae and the Sea, Ember Kearney was born with the mark of the Silver Stag. Rejected by both her bloodlines, she now works for the Wild Hunt as an investigator.

CAST OF CHARACTERS

- **Herne the Hunter:** Herne is the son of the Lord of the Hunt, Cernunnos, and Morgana, goddess of the Fae and the Sea. A demigod—given his mother's mortal beginnings—he's a lusty, protective god and one hell of a good boss. Owner of the Wild Hunt Agency, he helps keep the squabbles between the world of Light and Dark Fae from spilling over into the mortal realms.
- **Talia:** A harpy who long ago lost her powers, Talia is a top-notch researcher for the agency, and a longtime friend of Herne's.
- **Viktor:** Viktor is half-ogre, half-human. Rejected by his father's people (the ogres), he came to work for Herne some decades back.
- **Yutani:** A coyote shifter who is dogged by the Great Coyote, Yutani was driven out of his village over two hundred years before. He walks in the shadow of the trickster, and is the IT specialist for the company.

Ember's Friends, Family, & Enemies:

- **Aoife:** A priestess of Morgana who guards the Seattle portal to the goddess's realm.
- **Celia:** Yutani's aunt.
- **Danielle:** Herne's daughter, born to an Amazon named Myrna.
- **DJ Jackson:** Angel's little half-brother, DJ is half Wulfine—wolf shifter. He now lives with a foster family for his own protection.
- **Erica:** A Dark Fae police officer, friend of Viktor's.

- **Elatha:** Fomorian King; enemy of the Fae race.
- **George Shipman:** Puma shifter. Member of the White Peak Puma Pride.
- **Ginty McClintlock:** A dwarf. Owner of Ginty's Waystation Bar & Grill.
- **Louhia:** Witch of Pohjola.
- **Marilee:** A priestess of Morgana, Ember's mentor. Possibly human—unknown.
- **Meadow O'Ceallaigh:** Member of the magic-born; member of LOCK. Twin sister of Trefoil.
- **Myrna:** An Amazon who had a fling with Herne many years back, which resulted in their daughter Danielle.
- **Rafé Forrester:** Brother to Ulstair, Raven's late fiancé; Angel's boyfriend. Actor/fast-food worker, now clerks at the Wild Hunt Agency. Dark Fae.
- **Sheila:** Viktor's girlfriend. A kitchen witch; one of the magic-born. Geology teacher who volunteers at the Chapel Hill Homeless Shelter.
- **Trefoil O'Ceallaigh:** Member of the magic-born; member of LOCK. Twin brother of Meadow.
- **Unkai:** Leader of the Orhanakai clan in the forest of Y'Bain. Dark Fae—Autumn's Bane.

The Gods, the Luo'henkah, the Elemental Spirits, & Their Courts:

- **Arawn:** Lord of the Dead. Lord of the Underworld.
- **Brighid:** Goddess of Healing, Inspiration, and

Smithery. The Lady of the Fiery Arrows, "Exalted One."

- **The Cailleach:** One of the Luo'henkah, the heart and spirit of winter.
- **Cerridwen:** Goddess of the Cauldron of Rebirth. Dark harvest mother goddess.
- **Cernunnos:** Lord of the Hunt, god of the Forest and King Stag of the Woods. Together with Morgana, Cernunnos originated the Wild Hunt and negotiated the covenant treaty with both the Light and the Dark Fae. Herne's father.
- **Corra:** Ancient Scottish serpent goddess. Oracle to the gods.
- **Coyote, also: Great Coyote:** Native American trickster spirit/god.
- **Danu:** Mother of the Pantheon. Leader of the Tuatha de Dannan.
- **Ferosyn:** Chief healer in Cernunnos's Court.
- **Herne:** (see The Wild Hunt)
- **Isella:** One of the Luo'henkah. The Daughter of Ice (daughter of the Cailleach).
- **Kuippana (also: Kipa):** Lord of the Wolves. Elemental forest spirit; Herne's distant cousin. Trickster. Leader of the SuVahta, a group of divine elemental wolf shifters.
- **Lugh the Long Handed:** Celtic Lord of the Sun.
- **Mielikki:** Lady of Tapiola. Finnish goddess of the Hunt and the Fae. Mother of the Bear, Mother of Bees, Queen of the Forest.
- **Morgana:** Goddess of the Fae and the Sea, she was originally human but Cernunnos lifted her to deityhood. She agreed to watch over the Fae

who did not return across the Great Sea. Torn by her loyalty to her people and her loyalty to Cernunnos, she at times finds herself conflicted about the Wild Hunt. Herne's mother.

- **The Morrígan:** Goddess of Death and Phantoms. Goddess of the battlefield.
- **Pandora:** Daughter of Zeus, Emissary of Typhon, the Father of Dragons.
- **Sejun:** A counselor in Cernunnos's employ. Raven's therapist. Elven.
- **Tapio:** Lord of Tapiola. Mielikki's Consort. Lord of the Woodlands. Master of Game.

The Fae Courts:

- **Navane:** The court of the Light Fae, both across the Great Sea and on the eastside of Seattle, the latter ruled by **Névé**.
- **TirNaNog:** The court of the Dark Fae, both across the Great Sea and on the east side of Seattle, the latter ruled by **Saílle**.

The Force Majeure:

A group of legendary magicians, sorcerers, and witches. They are not human, but magic-born. There are twenty-one at any given time and the only way into the group is to be hand chosen, and the only exit from the group is death.

- **Merlin, The:** Morgana's father. Magician of ancient Celtic fame.
- **Taliesin:** The first Celtic bard. Son of

Cerridwen, originally a servant who underwent magical transformation and finally was reborn through Cerridwen as the first bard.

- **Ranna:** Powerful sorceress. Elatha's mistress.
- **Rasputin:** The Russian sorcerer and mystic.
- **Väinämöinen:** The most famous Finnish bard.

The Dragonni—the Dragon Shifters:

- The Celestial Wanders (Blue, Silver, and Gold Dragons)
- The Mountain Dreamers (Green and Black Dragons)
- The Luminous Warriors (White, Red, and Shadow Dragons)
- **Ashera:** A blue dragon
- **Aso:** White dragon, bound to Pandora, twin of Variance.
- **Echidna:** The Mother of Dragons (born of the Titans Gaia and Tartarus)
- **Typhon:** The Father of Dragons (born of the Titans Gaia and Tartarus).
- **Variance:** White Dragon, bound to Pandora, twin of Aso.

TIMELINE OF SERIES

Year 1:

- May/Beltane: **The Silver Stag** (Ember)
- June/Litha: **Oak & Thorns** (Ember)
- August/Lughnasadh: **Iron Bones** (Ember)
- September/Mabon: **A Shadow of Crows** (Ember)
- Mid-October: **Witching Hour** (Raven)
- Late October/Samhain: **The Hallowed Hunt** (Ember)
- December/Yule: **The Silver Mist** (Ember)

Year 2:

- January: **Witching Bones** (Raven)
- Late January–February/Imbolc: **A Sacred Magic** (Ember)
- March/Ostara: **The Eternal Return** (Ember)

TIMELINE OF SERIES

- May/Beltane: **Sun Broken** (Ember)
- June/Litha: **Witching Moon** (Raven)

PLAYLIST

I often write to music, and Witching Moon was no exception. Here's the playlist I used for this book.

- **Air:** Moon Fever; Playground Love; Napalm Love
- **Airstream:** Electra (Religion Cut)
- **Alexandros:** Milk (Bleach Version); Mosquito Bite
- **Alice in Chains:** Sunshine; Man in the Box; Bleed the Freak
- **Android Lust:** Here & Now; Saint Over
- **Band of Skulls:** I Know What I Am
- **The Black Angels:** Currency; Hunt Me Down; Death March; Indigo Meadow; Don't Play With Guns; Always Maybe; Black isn't Black
- **Black Mountain:** Queens Will Play
- **Blind Melon:** No Rain
- **Boom! Bap! Pow!:** Suit
- **Brandon & Derek Fiechter:** Night Fairies; Toll

Bridge; Will-O'-Wisps; Black Wolf's Inn; Naiad River; Mushroom Woods

- **The Bravery:** Believe
- **Broken Bells:** The Ghost Inside
- **Camouflage Nights:** (It Could Be) Love
- **Colin Foulke:** Emergence
- **Crazy Town:** Butterfly
- **Danny Cudd:** Double D; Remind; Once Again; Timelessly Free; To The Mirage
- **David Bowie:** Golden Years; Let's Dance; Sister Midnight; I'm Afraid of Americans; Jean Jeanie
- **Death Cab For Cutie:** I Will Possess Your Heart
- **Dizzi:** Dizzi Jig; Dance of the Unicorns
- **DJ Shah:** Mellomaniac
- **Don Henley:** Dirty Laundry; Sunset Grill; The Garden of Allah; Everybody Knows
- **Eastern Sun:** Beautiful Being
- **Eels:** Love of the Loveless; Souljacker Part 1
- **Elektrisk Gonnar:** Uknowhatiwant
- **FC Kahuna:** Hayling
- **The Feeling:** Sewn
- **Filter:** Hey Man Nice Shot
- **Finger Eleven:** Paralyzer
- **Flora Cash:** You're Somebody Else
- **Fluke:** Absurd
- **Foster The People:** Pumped Up Kicks
- **Garbage:** Queer; Only Happy When It Rains; #1Crush; Push It; I Think I'm Paranoid
- **Gary Numan:** Hybrid; Cars; Petals; Ghost Nation; My Name Is Ruin; Pray For The Pain You Serve; I Am Dust
- **Godsmack:** Voodoo

- **The Gospel Whisky Runners:** Muddy Waters
- **The Hang Drum Project:** Shaken Oak; St. Chartier
- **Hang Massive:** Omat Odat; Released Upon Inception; Thingless Things; Boat Ride; Transition to Dreams: End of Sky; Warmth of the Sun's Rays; Luminous Emptiness
- **The Hu:** The Gereg; Wolf Totem
- **Imagine Dragons:** Natural
- **In Strict Confidence:** Snow White; Tiefer; Silver Bullets; Forbidden Fruit
- **J Rokka:** Marine Migration
- **Jessica Bates:** The Hanging Tree
- **Korn:** Freak on a Leash; Make Me Bad
- **Lorde:** Yellow Flicker Beat; Royals
- **Low:** Witches; Nightingale; Plastic Cup; Monkey; Half-Light
- **M.I.A.:** Bad Girls
- **Many Rivers Ensemble:** Blood Moon; Oasis; Upwelling; Emergence
- **Marconi Union:** First Light; Alone Together; Flying (In Crimson Skies); Always Numb; Time Lapse; On Reflection; Broken Colours; We Travel; Weightless
- **Marilyn Manson:** Arma-Goddamn-Motherfucking-Geddon
- **Matt Corby:** Breathe
- **NIN:** Closer; Head Like A Hole; Terrible Lie; Sin (Long); Deep
- **Nirvana:** Lithium; About A Girl; Come As You Are; Lake of Fire; You Know You're Right
- **Orgy:** Social Enemies; Orgy

- **Pati Yang:** All That is Thirst
- **Puddle of Mudd:** Famous; Psycho
- **Red Venom:** Let's Get It On
- **Rob Zombie:** American Witch; Living Dead Girl; Never Gonna Stop
- **Rue du Soleil:** We Can Fly; Le Francaise; Wake Up Brother; Blues Du Soleil
- **Screaming Trees:** Where The Twain Shall Meet; All I Know
- **Shriekback:** Underwater Boys; Over the Wire; This Big Hush; Agony Box; Bollo Rex; Putting All The Lights Out; The Fire Has Brought Us Together; Shovelheads; And the Rain; Wiggle & Drone; Now These Days Are Gone; The King in the Tree
- **Spiderbait:** Shazam!
- **Tamaryn:** While You're Sleeping, I'm Dreaming; Violet's In A Pool
- **Thomas Newman:** Dead Already
- **Tom Petty:** Mary Jane's Last Dance
- **Trills:** Speak Loud
- **The Verve:** Bitter Sweet Symphony
- **Vive la Void:** Devil
- **Wendy Rule:** Let the Wind Blow
- **Yoshi Flower:** Brown Paper Bag

BIOGRAPHY

New York Times, Publishers Weekly, and USA Today bestselling author Yasmine Galenorn writes urban fantasy and paranormal romance, and is the author of more than sixty-five books, including the Wild Hunt Series, the Fury Unbound Series, the Bewitching Bedlam Series, the Indigo Court Series, and the Otherworld Series, among others. She's also written nonfiction metaphysical books. She is the 2011 Career Achievement Award Winner in Urban Fantasy, given by RT Magazine.

Yasmine has been in the Craft since 1980, is a shamanic witch and High Priestess. She describes her life as a blend of teacups and tattoos. She lives in Kirkland, WA, with her husband Samwise and their cats. Yasmine can be reached via her website at Galenorn.com.

Indie Releases Currently Available:

The Wild Hunt Series:
   The Silver Stag

Oak & Thorns
Iron Bones
A Shadow of Crows
The Hallowed Hunt
The Silver Mist
Witching Hour
Witching Bones
A Sacred Magic
The Eternal Return
Sun Broken
Witching Moon
Autumn's Bane

Whisper Hollow Series:
Autumn Thorns
Shadow Silence
The Phantom Queen

Bewitching Bedlam Series:
Bewitching Bedlam
Maudlin's Mayhem
Siren's Song
Witches Wild
Casting Curses
Demon's Delight
Bedlam Calling: A Bewitching Bedlam Anthology
The Wish Factor (a prequel short story)
Blood Music (a prequel novella)
Blood Vengeance (a Bewitching Bedlam novella)
Tiger Tails (a Bewitching Bedlam novella)

Fury Unbound Series:

Fury Rising
Fury's Magic
Fury Awakened
Fury Calling
Fury's Mantle

Indigo Court Series:
Night Myst
Night Veil
Night Seeker
Night Vision
Night's End
Night Shivers
Indigo Court Books, 1-3: Night Myst, Night Veil, Night Seeker (Boxed Set)
Indigo Court Books, 4-6: Night Vision, Night's End, Night Shivers (Boxed Set)

Otherworld Series:
Moon Shimmers
Harvest Song
Blood Bonds
Otherworld Tales: Volume 1
Otherworld Tales: Volume 2
For the rest of the Otherworld Series, see website at Galenorn.com.

Chintz 'n China Series:
Ghost of a Chance
Legend of the Jade Dragon
Murder Under a Mystic Moon
A Harvest of Bones

BIOGRAPHY

One Hex of a Wedding

Holiday Spirits

Chintz 'n China Books, 1 – 3: Ghost of a Chance,
Legend of the Jade Dragon, Murder Under A
Mystic Moon

Chintz 'n China Books, 4-6: A Harvest of Bones, One
Hex of a Wedding, Holiday Spirits

Bath and Body Series (originally under the name India
Ink):

Scent to Her Grave

A Blush With Death

Glossed and Found

Misc. Short Stories/Anthologies:

Once Upon a Kiss (short story: Princess Charming)

Once Upon a Curse (short story: Bones)

Once Upon a Ghost (short story: Rapunzel
Dreaming)

The Witching Hour (novel: Bewitching Bedlam)

After Midnight (novel: Fury Rising)

Magickal Nonfiction:

Embracing the Moon

Tarot Journeys

CPSIA information can be obtained
at www.ICGtesting.com
Printed in the USA
LVHW032132080321
680887LV00010B/2052